I phoned Sandy that night and explained about Dave. "What am I going to do?" I wailed. "I can't believe he has a girlfriend!"

"Let me think for a minute," she said, pausing. "Katie, I've got it! You're going to go to that party on Friday night. Work on your tan this week, and on Friday wear your sexiest swimsuit. Dave's relationship with Cindy is all in the past. He likes you, only he just hasn't realized it yet."

"Oh, I really don't—" I began to protest.

"Just listen," Sandy interrupted. "He thought you were pretty enough to find out more about you when he first saw you, so just wait until he sees you looking spectacular. Don't give up yet, Katie."

After I got off the phone, I started to think about Sandy's plan. It was one thing for her to say that I should look spectacular and another for me to do it. Maybe Dave wouldn't even notice me. Still, it *was* worth a try.

Special Someone

Terri Fields

BANTAM BOOKS
TORONTO • NEW YORK • LONDON • SYDNEY • AUCKLAND

To Rick, who makes every day
a special one

RL 6, IL age 11 and up

SPECIAL SOMEONE
A Bantam Book / October 1984
Reprinted 1985

Cover photo by Pat Hill

ISBN 0-553-24255-5

Published simultaneously in the United States and Canada

Bantam Books are published by Bantam Books, Inc. Its trademark,
consisting of the words ''Bantam Books'' and the portrayal of a
rooster, is registered in U.S. Patent and Trademark Office and in
other countries. Marca Registrada. Bantam Books, Inc., 666 Fifth
Avenue, New York, New York 10103.

Printed and bound in Great Britain by Hunt Barnard Printing Ltd.

O   0 9 8 7 6 5 4 3 2 1

Chapter One

How can my parents do this to me? I asked myself as I stared out the kitchen window, watching the heat waves bounce off the concrete sidewalk. *No wonder the only things that live in Arizona are snakes and cacti!* I sighed deeply, imagining what my friends were doing that day. They had probably driven up to one of the gorgeous Minnesota lakes and were having an absolutely great time, while I was stuck here in the middle of no place where it was boiling hot and I didn't know a soul. Boy, life sure was unfair!

Could it have been only two months before that my best friend, Sandy, had slept over and we'd plotted all kinds of wonderful summer plans? Sandy had sprawled comfortably across my bed. "Hey, Katie, the Elgin Cin-

1

ema is having an old movie series next month," she told me. "I saw the schedule. There are going to be some really good ones."

"Wow, that's great!" Sandy and I loved to see old movies together. "I bet Alice and Andy are excited about it, too."

"Alice says they've made a steady date for every Tuesday next month to go to the movies."

"Alice is lucky," I said almost to myself, "having a boyfriend who likes so many things that she does."

"Hey, don't sound so sad, Katie." Sandy swung her legs off the bed and came over to where I was sitting. "We'll meet some nice guys soon."

"Nice, sure," I answered. "The boys at school are nice. But most of them are so immature."

"I know what you mean," Sandy said. "They're so wrapped up in themselves they hardly listen to a word you say to them. It would be different with an older guy."

"That's what I think," I said softly. Sandy crossed back and flopped down on my bed again, and we were quiet for a moment.

"Oh, guess what," Sandy said, snapping her fingers. "Alice's parents said she could borrow their car anytime she wants; so we'll be able to go swimming a lot this summer."

"Ooh, I can't wait," I said and smiled. "There's nothing like an ice cold lake on a hot summer day. And there are so many beautiful places down Route Sixty-one. Grey Swan Pond is my favorite."

"And I know why, too," Sandy said, teasing me. "Because the kids from the university go up there all the time. You keep one eye on the swans and the other on the handsome college guys."

I ran over and gave Sandy a playful push. "Now does that sound like something I would do?" I asked innocently.

"Yes!" she said. "But don't worry. I'll be keeping my eyes open, too. It really would be fun to date an older guy for once."

"Mmm," I sighed. "Oh, Sandy, what a summer this could turn out to be!"

How those words came back to haunt me now. What a summer, indeed! Sandy and Alice and all my other friends were home in Minnesota, and I was thousands of miles away in an awful place called Tempe, Arizona, with no one but my parents to talk to. There'd be no old movie series, no lake swimming, no lying on the beach with Sandy and watching cute college guys.

3

I heard the key turn in the lock, and my parents entered the house speaking in hushed tones. That probably meant they were talking about me. Mom breezed into the kitchen, and I wondered how on earth she could look so cool and cheerful when it was at least 110 degrees outside, "Katie, I'm so glad you're home!" she exclaimed, ignoring the fact that I'd barely stuck my head out the door since we'd gotten to Tempe. "Dad has some wonderful news for you!"

"You mean we're leaving this place and going back to Minnesota?" I really didn't mean to say it, it just popped out of my mouth.

Mom gave me a look that I knew all too well. "Katie Thompson! How can you be so selfish. I'm so proud of your father, and you should be, too. Just get it through your head that we aren't going home until the end of the summer!" She looked really exasperated, started to say something else, and then just stopped, sighed, and said, "Oh, Katie, please just make the best of being here."

Dad walked into the kitchen, said hi, and continued on to the living room. I followed him. Well, I *was* proud of him. He really was one of the smartest men in the U.S., and I'm not saying that just because he's my father. In fact, we were in Tempe because he'd been asked to teach a special economics seminar at Arizona State University that summer. People had come from all over the country to learn from him.

He looked tired that night, and as he sank into his easy chair in the living room, he ran his hand through his graying hair. Setting his tortoiseshell glasses on the coffee table, Dad looked up at me and said, "Well, princess"— that was his pet name for me—"I know you've been unhappy so far this summer, and I think I've got some news that will make you feel a whole lot better. How would you like a summer job?"

My heart began to race, and I could feel my face flush. How would I like a summer job? That was like asking how I'd like to be able to eat banana splits every single day without ever getting fat! Dad knew that my goal someday was to open Katie's Clothing Boutique. We'd talked about it many times, and although he'd said he was glad I already had a career in mind, he was dead set against my finding a part-time job so that I could start getting some experience in running a store. Every time I brought the subject up, Dad would tell me that I was too young for a job, and that was that. Now, he was actually giving me the go-ahead!

Dad continued, "Jim Tohn owns the drugstore right across from the university campus, and he needs a new cashier. I had a nice talk with him, and he agreed to hire you, on my strong recommendation," he added, smiling. "If you want the job, you start tomorrow morning at eight-forty-five." His blue eyes twinkled. "I hope you don't mind. I told him you'd be there."

I leaned over and hugged my father tightly. "Just try to keep me away!" I exclaimed. "Dad, you are terrific!"

The rest of the night flew by. First, I wrote Sandy a letter telling her the good news. Then I went through my wardrobe, looking for something to wear that would make me look professional. Thank goodness one of the few skirts I'd brought with me looked fairly grown-up.

Needless to say, it was impossible for me to go to sleep, and after tossing and turning the whole night, I finally gave up at six in the morning. I, Katie Thompson, was finally going to leave childhood behind and have a real job. Of course, it wasn't in a clothing store, which would have been my first choice, but I could still study the displays and figure out what made people buy things in the drugstore. Someday I was going to have the fanciest boutique in all of Minneapolis, and anyone who wanted just the right clothes would come to my store. This was the first step toward making my dream come true.

I dressed slowly, trying hard to picture University Drugs in my mind. Fortunately it was one of the few stores I'd been in since we'd come here. I closed my eyes, but I just couldn't remember that much about the store. If only I'd known that I'd be working there one day, I'd have paid more attention. All I remembered was that it was fairly large and kind of old-fashioned and that the aisles were cluttered with goods. *Well*, I told myself, *you'll know more about it soon enough.*

As I combed my hair, I stared in the mirror. My green eyes stared unhappily back. I looked like such a baby. The college kids who came in the store to buy things would probably ask me where my mother was. I wished I were taller than five feet one. With a father taller than six feet, it didn't seem fair that I was so short. People always thought I was younger than sixteen. I piled my light brown hair on top of my head in a bun; I looked like an old lady. I tried a short ponytail, but that made me look too young. Finally, I pulled back a thin strand from each side of my head and fastened them together with a barette. I didn't look like a college student, but at least it was pretty.

Mom and Dad called for me to come and join them for breakfast, but the thought of eating was more than I could bear. My stomach was doing flip-flops. At eight-fifteen I couldn't stand it any more, and I said goodbye to my parents, then began walking to the drugstore. I knew I was way too early, but I just couldn't stand around another moment. We were renting a house only a few blocks from the campus, so I wandered down the road a little to kill enough time to arrive at exactly eight-forty-five.

I got to the door of University Drugs just as Mr. Tohn was unlocking it. He was an older man, bald, with glasses, and his mouth was set in a firm half-smile. Taking a deep breath, I hoped for the best. "Hi," I said, "I'm Katie Thompson. Thanks for hiring me. It's so terrific to have a job. Uh—I mean, it's nice to be working for you. I mean, I know I'll really like it here." Mr. Tohn just looked at me. He had to think I was a real jerk, babbling away like that. Why did I have to get so nervous?

Mr. Tohn motioned me into the store, and we walked in silence toward the cash register. He showed me all the store procedures, and I took notes. There were so many things to remember that I just prayed I could keep them all straight. Mr. Tohn said that he'd be around and told me to ask him if I got confused about anything. But I hoped I wouldn't have to, especially after his parting comment. He lifted his glasses, rubbed the bridge of his nose, and then ran his hand over his balding head. "Katie," he said, "there is one other thing I should tell you. I admire your father very much. He's a brilliant man, and it's a credit to the university that he's teaching here. I've been an active alumnus of ASU for years, and I hired you because your father asked me to. But I have a long list of college kids who want the job, and if you can't do it right, it doesn't matter who your father is, I'll hire someone else." Mr. Tohn walked away, and over his shoulder he called, "Good luck." He flipped the store sign from "closed" to "open."

Boy, I thought, *I'll need all the luck I can get!*

People streamed in to the store all morning, and there was a line at my register in almost no time. I certainly wasn't going to get a chance to break in to this job slowly. *Charge tax on pencils, don't charge tax on candy*, I told myself. It wasn't easy to keep the key and category straight for every single item. Checking my notes often, I hoped Mr. Tohn wouldn't think I was too slow. I wanted to keep this job more than anything.

The faces that passed me were just blurs, and by closing time I realized that I had been concentrating so hard I would never have noticed if anyone thought I was too young to have the job. As I counted out the money in the cash register, my heart was in my mouth. What if it didn't balance with the amount on the register tape? Would Mr. Tohn fire me on the spot? I counted my money twice and found with relief that it did balance.

I took everything to Mr. Tohn and waited patiently. He put on his glasses and scrutinized the money and receipts very carefully. "Well, you have two overrings, but I see that you did balance out. That's not bad for your first day. I think, Ms. Thompson, that you may just make it here!"

Not exactly glowing praise, but I floated home as if someone had just given me a key to the whole world. For once I hardly noticed the Arizona heat. I unlocked the front door and stepped into the cool living room. "I had a really great day!" I shouted. No one answered; Mom and Dad weren't home yet. I went into the kitchen and got myself an ice cold glass of orange juice. I was bursting to tell someone about my new job. Almost instinctively I reached for the telephone. Then I realized that I didn't know a single soul to call. *Well,* I thought smugly, *all that may just change now that I'm working! I bet I'll meet tons of college kids at the store.* In the meantime I couldn't wait to share news this great, and so I got some stationery and sat down at the desk in my room to begin a letter to Sandy.

Dear Sandy,

Guess what? I got a job—as a cashier in a drugstore! I feel so grown-up. I don't think the owner of the store really thought I could handle the job, but I did it. I kept track of everything, and he seemed really pleased, even though he doesn't show much emotion. Boy, do I ever wish you were here so that I could tell you everything in detail.

Sandy, I was so scared that the college kids would realize that I'm only sixteen and resent me for having this job, but no one said anything at all. Today was so busy that I didn't get a chance to pay much attention to any of the people, but overall, they seemed nice. As soon as I'm more certain of what I'm doing on the register, I'm going to try to meet some of the college kids. I may even flirt with some of the guys! Watch out, Sandy! I'm

going to have that mature older boyfriend
we talked about at home.

Love,
Katie

I heard the front door open and put my
pen down. Mom and Dad were home, and I
was bursting to tell them all about my job. I
ran into the living room. "Boy, am I ever happy
today!" I yelled and launched into a moment-
by-moment account of my day. My parents listened to every detail and really seemed
interested. "You know, this summer is sure
full of surprises," I said. "Just a couple of
months ago I thought I'd be spending the
summer swimming in Minnesota. And now
I'm nowhere near home, and I have a job! I just
know that working is going to be great. I've
decided to keep a sketchbook of ideas for
Katie's Clothing Boutique."

Dad laughed and ruffled my hair. "Well,
princess, this certainly is a different girl from
the sourpuss who's been greeting me. I'm glad
you like the job so much, and I've got a feeling
Mr. Tohn will have himself a darn good
employee."

I felt just as excited and not nearly so
nervous as I began my second day at Univer-

sity Drugs. I opened the register just as Mr. Tohn had shown me the day before. He wandered over a few minutes before nine to help me do it, and I proudly told him I'd already finished the job. He looked over my shoulder to check what I'd done. "Hmm, good for you, young lady," he mumbled. That was all he said, but I could tell he was impressed.

That day things weren't so strange, and I began to put faces together with the candy bars, toothpastes, and magazines that were being thrust at the register. I smiled at one girl. "Go ahead and get that candy bar. It's made of a special chocolate that has no calories in it," I said teasingly.

"Great," she said and laughed. "Then I'll buy two."

I was feeling wonderful. The college kids were actually accepting me! OK, so I hadn't spoken to a guy yet. But for now, it was more than enough just to admire them as they walked through the store. They seemed so much more at ease and self-assured than the high-school boys at home.

"I can't decide," a voice said, interrupting my thoughts, "between an O'Henry bar or a Milky Way. If you were me, which would you get?" A tall, dark-haired guy wearing an ASU T-shirt was standing by the register.

"Oh, the Milky Way. I've never liked O'Henry bars much." I smiled at him.

"OK," he said, grinning, "that settles it. You look like you have good taste. I'll buy the Milky Way." He paid and left.

Yippee, I thought. *I've just had my first conversation with a college guy.* Even if it hadn't been a big deal, at least I hadn't frozen. I'd actually talked to him, and he was nice.

Boy, I sure wished Sandy were there to share my new adventures. The day before I'd started my first job, and that day I'd talked to a college guy. I had the feeling that this was going to be a very interesting summer.

Chapter Two

What the next day brought was absolutely the most perfect boy that any girl could ever hope to see. He walked in the door of the drugstore, and the whole place seemed to take on a special glow. *Please*, I silently whispered, *don't leave without coming close enough so that I can at least get a good look at your face.*

He wandered through the store in no particular hurry, and my eyes followed his every move. *Don't be so obvious*, I warned myself, and though it just about killed me, I made myself look away from him. The store was unusually empty, and I allowed my mind to drift. What would it be like to go out with a boy like that? He'd have to be kind and considerate, I was sure, a great listener, understanding, sensitive. I had settled deeply into a super daydream when a voice interrupted me.

"Wow, anyone that deep in thought must be thinking about something pretty important."

I blushed and looked up. It was him. And he was actually standing in front of the register talking to me. Up close, he was even better looking than he had been from far away. He had blond, curly hair and penetrating blue eyes. And that smile! He was the most handsome boy I'd ever seen.

"Uh-oh," he said, "I think the lady is fading off again."

"C-can I help you?" I stuttered.

"Well, I'd kind of like to buy this candy bar," he answered. I looked down and realized that he had been holding an Almond Joy in his hand, probably for the whole time I'd been daydreaming. Why was it that with everyone else I'd been pleasant and efficient, but then, when it really counted, I was acting like a real space cadet?

I smiled weakly and hit a key to ring up his purchase, but I was so nervous that I hit thirty-five dollars instead of thirty-five cents. I felt like a total fool. I couldn't even apologize. The words just stuck in my throat. The boy waited patiently while I voided the sale and rang it up again. Dropping the coins on the counter, he smiled that perfect smile again, and then he was gone.

Boy, Katie, I told myself sarcastically, *you're handling these college kids just fine. The most terrific boy in the whole world comes in to this store to buy one simple candy bar, and do you talk to him, do you impress him with your great sense of humor? Nope, you just fall apart!*

At home, Sandy and I used to act out imaginary scenes with boys. We were always very clever and charming, and they always fell madly in love with us. So much for all our fantasies. I mean, here was a guy in living flesh, who was better than anyone Sandy and I had ever made up, and my conversation with him hadn't been impressive at all, it had been positively moronic.

The day dragged by slowly. I kept watching the window to see if *he* might be coming back, and every time I saw a tall guy with blond, curly hair in the distance, my hopes would rise. Then, as a stranger passed by, my heart would sink. Some moments I thought I'd give anything to have him walk back into the store, and others, I figured that it probably wouldn't matter. I'd only mess things up again.

For the next few days, I tried everything to get that guy off my mind. I told myself I was being silly. I had no idea what he was like or even what his name was. After all, I wasn't some boy-crazy girl who flipped over every guy she met. But the harder I tried to think about other things, the more I could think only of him. To tell the truth, it was absolutely wearing me out.

I trudged home one evening to find a letter from Sandy. I got a glass of lemonade, then plopped down into a chair and started reading. "Dear Katie," it began. "Everyone here thinks you're really lucky to have that job. It's the perfect excuse to be around college guys. We're so jealous, we could just die."

Boy, Sandy, I said to myself, *if you only knew that I've already blown everything.*

Sandy told me in her letter about all the waterskiing and swimming she was doing. She described in detail a big party Alice had thrown. "I went with reliable old Kenny," she said. "He's not too exciting, but he's always around. But I'm sure he's nothing compared to the gorgeous college guys you're probably meeting. I can't tell you how much I'd love to trade places with you for the weekend."

"Sure, Sandy," I said out loud to the empty room. "If you were me, you would have no dates for this weekend and absolutely nothing to do." I crumpled up her letter and tossed it at the wastebasket. It missed. Typical of my luck all day.

Well, it wasn't going to do me much good to sit around and feel sorry for myself. All I could do was try to forget about my mystery man and make the most of my job. Easier said than done, but I could at least give it a try. Some extra projects would help occupy my time.

The next day at work I asked Mr. Tohn if I could rearrange the display in one of the store windows. "I'd do it on my own time," I said, "I mean, you wouldn't have to pay me extra or anything. I've got some great ideas for using the stuffed animals that are just sitting in that old chicken wire box up front."

Actually, I didn't have any specific plans, but then I never really expected Mr. Tohn to agree to the project. But to my surprise, he did.

"Katie," he said, "you've shown a lot of initiative since you've started here. I'll tell you what. You can work on the arrangement whenever business is slow. Save receipts for the supplies you buy, and I'll pay you back for up to twenty dollars worth of material." Then, typical for him, he added, "That display had better be good, or you'll come in on your own time and take it apart."

I smiled to myself. I was learning that Mr. Tohn really was quite a nice man under his gruff exterior.

The rest of the day I used any spare time to draw sketches of my display. I wanted it to be eye-catching. It was fun just to think about it, and I couldn't wait to see if the results would mean more sales of stuffed animals. No matter what, it would be a good learning experience, another step toward Katie's Clothing Boutique.

Most of the time I concentrated on my display plan or the customers, many of whom were beginning to call me by my name. But to be honest, I have to admit that I couldn't help letting my eyes stray to the window to see if my mystery man was anywhere around, and I couldn't stop my heart from pounding whenever I saw a tall boy with curly, blond hair in the distance.

It's strange the way life goes because when he finally did come back into the store, things were so hectic I didn't even notice that he was there. A large display of aspirin had gotten knocked over, and I'd been trying to put it back together again when there was a big rush of customers. The store was full of people, and everyone was late for class. I was ringing things up so quickly that I felt like a part of the cash register.

Finally the last customer in line left, and standing off to the side, watching me and smiling, was my mystery guy! At first I thought I was imagining him. He ambled over to me, and his smile seemed to fill the whole store. "Ah-ha," he laughed. "I see that the girl with the pretty green eyes has been too busy today to do any deep thinking."

I could hardly believe my luck as it registered that he'd said I had pretty green eyes *Katie, I told myself, if you mess this up, you don't deserve another chance at anything in your entire lifetime!*

I smiled, a little nervously, and prayed silently that I still had some mascara on. Trying to sound casual and offhand, I replied, "The girl with the pretty green eyes is named Katie, and who is the guy with the curly, blond hair?"

There was that smile again. "Katie," he said thoughtfully. "It fits you perfectly. I'm Dave, and I can guarantee that I'll be back soon to see those eyes again." Then he turned and walked out the door.

I wanted to shout with joy. He came back! And he said he wanted to see me again! I was so excited that I wasn't watching what I was doing and accidentally hit an open box of foil-wrapped mint patties, and they went flying. I dashed around the counter to pick them up before Mr. Tohn noticed. But the world was perfect. A few dented mint patties didn't matter.

Chapter Three

Every word of the conversation I'd had with Dave was etched on my brain, and my pen could hardly keep up with my thoughts as I got it all down in a letter to Sandy. Lying on my bed, stationery propped up in front of me, I scribbled furiously.

Dear Sandy,

   If only you could see him! I hope I'll be able to send you a picture of him soon, but in the meantime I'll just have to describe him to you. Dave is about six feet tall, with a fantastic tan. I bet he likes sports because he sure has a great build. His eyes are so blue I can hardly believe it, and with his blond, curly hair and terrific smile, he'd make your heart stop, too. Can you picture him?

I was so incredibly happy when he came into the store today. Best of all, I know that he was purposely waiting for a chance to talk to me. Stay tuned. I've got a feeling that you'll be hearing more real soon.

Hugs,
Katie

I reread the letter and sighed to myself. How could I ever have thought this would be the worst summer of my life? Each day was turning out to be more exciting than the last. It was still early, but I started getting ready for bed, anyway. The sooner I went to sleep, the sooner the next day would come and then maybe I'd see Dave again. My emotions had me worn out, and I fell asleep quickly. I bet I smiled all night long.

The next morning I was up early. I took about an hour going through my clothes to find an outfit that would make my eyes look their greenest. I began to wonder if instead of saving all my pay for school clothes I should get a few new summer clothes, too. Finally I chose a green-and-white print dress. It looked pretty with my eyes and hair. I felt kind of

dressed up since most of the college girls I'd
seen wore only shorts or cutoffs. I wanted to
look special for Dave. Besides, Mr. Tohn said
he didn't care how casual everyone else looked
or how hot it got, his employees were to be
neatly dressed.

I brushed my hair until it was full and
shiny. Carefully I put on a touch of bronze eye
shadow and then added just the right amount
of mascara. I surveyed myself in the mirror.
Not bad, but I looked pale. Everyone in
Arizona had such great tans. I guessed, from
what I'd overheard at work, that that was
because most social life took place around
swimming pools.

I started to daydream. Dave and I were sitting by the edge of a pool, dangling our feet in
the cool water and holding tall glasses of lemonade. "To you, Katie, the perfect girl," Dave
whispered as we clicked glasses together.
Mmm, just thinking about it gave me the
chills. I could hardly wait to see him.

My mind clicked into panic. What time
was it, anyway? I ran into the kitchen to look
at the clock. Eight-forty-five—I should have
left fifteen minutes before. I rushed out the
door and ran to work. I could feel the perspiration ruining my makeup and my hair slipping
from the carefully arranged combs.

Trying not to show my breathlessness, I walked in through the door two minutes before opening. Mr. Tohn looked at me with one raised eyebrow, but he didn't say anything. It was the latest I'd ever gotten to work, and we both knew it.

Feeling guilty, I resolved to do an extra good job that morning. Dave probably wouldn't stop by until the afternoon, anyway. That was when he'd come in the other two times. By the time the clock approached two, I'd managed to clean the candy rack, straighten the vitamins, and still take care of all the customers. *That ought to make up for being late*, I thought.

I took out the notebook I was using for my designs for the stuffed animal display. I'd thought it would be so easy. I'd rejected not only my first idea, but the next five as well. It was depressing. I was determined to come up with something perfect, and the best I'd been able to come up with was just OK.

I sighed dejectedly. I was too nervous to think about the display anymore. After all, Dave would be coming in any minute now. I still couldn't figure out quite why I was reacting so strongly to Dave. I wasn't the kind of girl who fell in love every week. Sure, I'd had a few crushes before, but no one had ever made me feel like Dave had. The rational part of me kept telling myself to quit letting my emotions run away with me. I mean, what did I know about this guy? Maybe he'd just been casually flirting with me. But another part of me refused to listen. It was that part that kept scanning the door with each passing hour. Thank goodness the afternoon was really busy. That distracted me at least a little bit.

Mr. Tohn had let me check in an order of merchandise, and it made me realize how much was involved in running a business. The shampoo part of the order hadn't come in, and Mr. Tohn was upset. He explained that it meant we could lose a lot of business—and not only in shampoo. If kids had to go elsewhere to buy shampoo, they'd pick up candy, film, and other items while they were there.

I was listening to the end of his explanation when out of the corner of my eye, I saw Dave walk into the store. He had come back! He did want to see me! I tried to seem interested in Mr. Tohn's words, but inwardly I begged him to finish quickly. What if Dave figured I was going to be tied up for a while and left?

Though it seemed like an eternity, it was really only a matter of minutes before Mr. Tohn finished his explanation and walked toward the back of the store. I thought Dave would come to the register immediately, but instead, he ambled over and glanced through the magazine rack. My "pretty green eyes" were willing him to come over to the register. But he didn't. Well, I wasn't going over to him. I refused to look like I was chasing him.

At that moment a group of college girls came in to pick up their developed film. Two of them couldn't find their film receipts, so they were standing before me searching through their purses. They totally blocked my view of Dave, and I wished I could tell them all just to go away. Of course I didn't, and in no time it seemed as if they'd dumped half the contents of their purses out on the counter, looking for the elusive receipts. Finally, they gave up, and I filled out lost-film receipt forms for them to sign for each roll of film. It seemed to take forever, but at last the girls had their pictures, and I had run the charges into the register. I wiped the perspiration from my forehead and glanced toward the magazine rack. Thank goodness, Dave was still standing there. He picked up a copy of the afternoon paper and brought it toward the register. *Boy, is this guy ever cool*, I thought. *He makes it all look so casual with the newspaper.*

Putting the paper on the counter, he

yawned and said almost to himself that it had been a very long day. His gaze never even brushed over me. Suddenly I wasn't so sure that it was an act. In fact, I wasn't sure he even remembered who I was or that he'd even spoken to me before. He put thirty cents on the counter for the paper.

"Thanks, Dave," I said, hoping to jar his memory.

He smiled, looked at me with recognition at last, and said, "I'm starved. I think I'll head for Pizza Pleasers. If you're off soon, why don't you join me?" While I was trying to get over my shock at his sudden change in attitude and come up with a casual acceptance, he started toward the door. Then, almost as an afterthought, he turned and asked, "See you there?"

"Sure," I replied shakily with what I hoped was an air of nonchalance. To myself, I silently yelled, *Yea*! In just fifteen minutes I would be sitting across from Dave, sharing a pizza with him. It wasn't just some made-up fantasy, he really did want to be with me!!

By five-thirty I had completely checked out the register. Luckily everything had balanced, and I didn't have to waste time going over it again. I gave Mr. Tohn the day's money and receipts and headed for the restroom. Looking in the mirror, I reapplied my mascara and eye shadow and straightened my clothes. OK, so I was stalling. But I was scared. I mean I'd never actually talked to Dave except for those few minutes in the store. What if, when I was sitting across the table from him, we couldn't keep a conversation going? I took a deep breath and walked toward the front door of the store, my sandals clicking against the wooden floor.

"Have a good time," called Mr. Tohn. "By the way, their pizza isn't bad." I blushed. I'd had no idea Mr. Tohn had heard my conversation with Dave. I was beginning to realize that not very much got past that man.

With a mixture of nervousness and excitement, I walked the block and a half to Pizza Pleasers. Outside the restaurant I hesitated a moment, then grabbed the large black handle and pulled open the heavy oak door. The smell of pizza was overwhelming, and in spite of my certainty that I wouldn't be able to eat a thing around Dave, my stomach growled. Standing in the entrance, I waited for my eyes to adjust to the semidarkness and hoped I'd hear him call my name. *Maybe he doesn't see me*, I thought, scanning the tables. The place was crowded, and I couldn't see Dave. Just as I was really beginning to feel like a fool standing in the doorway, I saw him wave to me from a corner booth.

As I walked up to his table, I noticed that the pizza was already there and Dave was eating. I wished he'd waited for me, but then he smiled, and I told myself that it didn't matter.

"Have a seat," he said. "Hope you don't mind that I started already, but I was starving. I wasn't sure of what you'd like, so I ordered black olive because that's what I like."

"Sure, that's just great," I lied, remembering all the times I'd picked the black olives out of pizzas my dad had ordered. But what did food matter? It was enough just to be sitting across the table from Dave.

"So, you like working at the drugstore?"

"I really love it. I mean, I'm learning so much." Then I caught myself. It wouldn't do to sound like a little kid all excited over her first job.

But Dave took it all in. "That's great. It's nice to talk to someone who's having a good summer." Dave cut himself another piece of pizza.

"Does that mean yours hasn't been so good?" I asked. I have to admit, I was hoping he'd say something like his summer was getting better now that he'd met me, but then I always was a big daydreamer.

"My summer has been terrible!" Dave complained. "I had a chance to go to Colorado with some friends and stay in the mountains for a few weeks. I really wanted to go, but I'm switching majors, so I needed to stay and pick up some credits this summer."

"Gee, that's tough." I hoped I sounded properly sympathetic. But secretly I was elated that the conversation was flowing so easily.

"Yeah, and the toughest thing is having Dr. Heke for European history." Dave went on to explain all his problems in great detail. I was fascinated. This was college from a whole different perspective from the one I had from my father. Dave talked for almost an hour, and I only interrupted him with sympathetic murmurs. Actually I was having a great time just looking at Dave's handsome face across the table. I'd even lost track of the time. I had no idea we'd been talking so long until a waitress walked up with the check and said that her shift had ended and could we please pay our bill.

I knew I had to get home soon or at least let my folks know what time to expect me. First, though, I wanted to find out if Dave had any further plans for us for the evening, but I didn't feel comfortable just coming right out and asking him. So I said, in what I hoped was a casual tone, "Tell you what, you paid for dinner, so if you come back to my place, I'll make us sundaes for dessert." I crossed my fingers and hoped he'd say yes. The thought of spending an entire evening with Dave was delicious.

"Thanks, Katie," he said, smiling, "but I've got to get back to the library. Maybe another time." He got up, and I followed him to the door. Dave opened it for me, and a blast of hot air hit us both. "Phew," he said, "the Arizona summer! Wish we were heading for a swimming pool, but it's off to hit the books for me." He reached one arm across my shoulders and pulled me toward him for a moment. "This was fun. We'll have to do it again." He winked, then walked away.

I stood watching Dave's tall, well-built physique move farther and farther away. I hoped he'd turn around and call out that he'd changed his mind, but he kept walking, and pretty soon he turned a corner, and I couldn't see him at all.

I walked home replaying my date with Dave. Wow, my first date with a college guy. And I hadn't had any trouble with the conversation. Actually, it hadn't been hard at all since Dave had done most of the talking. I was glad, too. Since he'd hardly asked anything about me, I'd never had to tell him I was only in high school. Still, there *were* a lot of things I would have liked to have told him, but I'd never had the chance. Oh, well, there'd be other dates with him, I hoped.

Deep in thought, I walked slowly home. When I opened the door, Mom called, "Katie, why are you so late? Were you working on your display? I left some dinner in the oven."

I followed the sound of Mom's voice into the bedroom. Dad was stretched out on the bed reading the newspaper, and Mom was sitting in an armchair with a book in her lap. "I'm not really hungry tonight. I stopped in at the pizza place near the drugstore with a guy I met."

"Oh?" Mom questioned invitingly. That was one thing I loved about her. She never pried, but she always let me know that the door was open if I wanted to discuss anything with her. Well, I wasn't ready to discuss Dave, yet.

I put the food Mom had saved for me in the refrigerator and considered writing to Sandy. I decided to wait a day or two and see if Dave asked me for another date. I plopped down in front of the TV set and watched a rerun of "Happy Days." Things certainly were easier for teenagers on TV. Everything was always resolved in a half hour's time.

Chapter Four

Well, I wish I could say that Dave became a part of my life immediately, but unfortunately he didn't. In fact, it was almost a whole week before he came into the drugstore again. During that week, I felt really frustrated. I realized that I didn't even know his last name, nor he mine, and that if I quit working at University Drugs, I'd probably never see him again. I knew that he liked black olives on pizza, and I had all the details of his problems with summer school, but I didn't know if I'd ever get a chance to be with him again. I didn't know how he felt about me or what he enjoyed doing with a girlfriend. It was almost funny—I knew everything except the things I most wanted to know.

When he did come back into the store, I

saw him out of the corner of my eye the minute he walked through the door, and my heart began to beat faster. He waited until the line at the register had cleared, then he came over to me. "Katie," he exclaimed as if he were almost surprised to see me. "How about if we meet at Pizza Pleasers tonight?"

Maybe I should have said no or asked him why he hadn't come to see me sooner, but once again I found myself enchanted by his penetrating blue eyes and gorgeous smile. Half an hour later I was sitting across from him, a large pizza with black olives in front of us. At first, I was absolutely resolved to find out more about who he was and what he really thought about me. But to tell the truth, I was so glad just to be with him again that I felt my resolve begin to disappear almost the minute we sat down. Still, I did give it a try before it was altogether gone. "Do you realize, Dave, that I know your major, but I still don't know your last name?"

"Miss Katie," he said, joking, "may I formally present Dave Cosburn." He stood and gave a slight bow.

"Charmed to meet you I'm sure," I kidded back, "and I go by the title of Katie Thompson." We both laughed. Then there was kind of a long silence, and, anxious to break it, I said, "Uhhh, Dave, how are things with Dr. Heke?"

"You wouldn't believe the way he's piling on the reading." He sighed, and I had to admit that he did look kind of tired. He ran a hand through his hair. "I don't know," he continued. "I've got to get top-notch grades. I mean, the competition to get into law school gets worse every year, and it's already impossible right now."

It was as if a dam to Dave's troubling thoughts had broken open, and he just talked and talked. He barely touched the pizza. His eyes locked into mine as he spoke, and I felt very close to him. He talked about how he studied four or five hours a night and how even that wasn't enough for Dr. Heke. Finally, he said that he really had to get back to the library.

As much as I wanted to, I didn't try to stop him. I knew he needed to go. My heart ached for him. How awful to have a dream you wanted that much and to be so afraid you'd never get it. I felt pretty selfish. Here I'd been worried about why he hadn't come back to see me sooner, while he was worrying about losing his whole future.

"Dave," I said earnestly. "You're going to make a terrific lawyer. Don't let that dumb Dr.

Heke get to you. You'll show him. I know you're going to do just great in his class."

As we walked out the door of the pizza parlor, our bodies were so close we were almost touching. It felt absolutely wonderful, and I hated the thought of having it end so soon.

"Dave," I said quickly before I could chicken out, "I've got a great idea. I'll go with you to the library. Then whenever you're ready to take a study break, we'll go for ice cream."

"But," he answered, "you don't even have your books. What could you possibly get done? Katie, you've been a big help, but I don't want you feeling sorry for me. Go have some fun!" He blew me a kiss. "Thanks, you're terrific!"

And again Dave was gone. *Darn*, I thought to myself. *I should have insisted on going with him.* I headed for home, then impulsively turned and started walking toward the old brick library. My heart was pounding. The building's entrance loomed in front of me, and I hesitantly pushed open the heavy glass doors. The place was huge. I felt totally overwhelmed. I saw a large sign that read Information, and I wished I could go up to the man sitting under it and say, "Excuse me, I need information about how to find Dave Cosburn."

Walking around the first floor, I saw college kids at every table. One couple was sitting very, very close together. I had the feeling that they weren't getting much studying done. Other kids seemed totally absorbed in their books. Dave was nowhere to be seen. I looked toward the elevator, but my courage was quickly ebbing away. What if he got mad at being interrupted while he was studying?

Call me a coward, but I decided that I'd rather savor the time we'd had together than risk ruining the whole evening, so I pushed the glass doors open again and headed home. As I walked I wished I had someone to talk to. I'd send Sandy a letter again soon, but writing just wasn't the same as having my friend to talk to and to help me figure out some things.

When I got home, Dad called out, "Princess, we've been waiting for you. Come celebrate. We're going out for hot fudge sundaes for dessert. Personally, I'm going to get a whole extra dish of whipped cream!"

"What's going on?" I asked, looking at the two champagne glasses sitting on the kitchen table. I had called my mom to tell her I wouldn't be home for dinner, but she hadn't mentioned that anything special had happened.

"Your father has just gotten word that his paper has been chosen as the keynote speech at the convention of the American Economic Association," Mom said, beaming.

"I know a great ice-cream parlor," Dad said, smiling. "It's right on campus, and the ice cream is really creamy." Dad's graying hair was slightly messy, and his glasses were perched atop his head. With his shirt-sleeves rolled up and the delighted grin on his face, he didn't look very scholarly. But I could see what had made Mom fall in love with him. It was really romantic the way she shared completely in his excitement. I wondered if I'd ever have that kind of relationship with anyone. I certainly hoped so.

Soon we were sitting in a cozy, homey, little ice-cream parlor. Outside, there were red-and white-striped awnings over the windows, and inside, white wrought-iron tables and chairs were crowded together. *Oh, please,* I silently prayed, *don't let Dave see me on campus eating ice cream with my parents.* I mean, I wanted them all to meet, but not that way. I still hadn't even told Dave that I wasn't a college student. Of course I would, I was just waiting for the right moment.

I ordered a chocolate almond hot fudge sundae with extra nuts and whipped cream, and my parents got sundaes, too.

"You know, Dad, I'd really like to hear you teach one of your classes," I said as we waited for our ice cream to arrive.

"Katie, I'd love to have you. You name the date and time. Why the sudden interest?"

"Well," I said teasingly, "I want to hear you before you're so famous that it's too crowded to get a seat."

"I don't think you have to worry about that." Dad laughed. "Speaking of famous, how is that stuffed animal display coming along—when do Mom and I get to see it? Ah, here come our sundaes, and, boy, do they look fantastic."

I sighed. "It isn't coming along very well. I don't know. Somehow, none of my ideas seem good enough to go ahead with."

Dad and Mom looked at each other. "You know," Dad said, digging into the mound of ice cream in front of him, "I've found that sometimes people try too hard to make everything perfect, and then they never get anything done."

There was silence; and then my mom changed the subject. "Katie," said Mom, "you don't have to go out for dinner with your friend. You know your friends are always welcome at home. You haven't invited anyone over since we've been in Arizona."

I knew that both my parents were concerned about me, and I could feel myself begin to blush. "Dad, I will get the display done. Mom, I just don't know anyone here that well. As soon as I do, I'll bring them home."

Mom should only have known how very much I wished I were bringing a certain someone home. I was beginning to think that this relationship with Dave was never going to go anywhere—other than Pizza Pleasers for an hour every so often. I'd be ninety-five and still waiting for him to kiss me. I was tempted to discuss the whole thing with Mom, but somehow I felt I ought to be able to handle it myself. After all, college girls didn't have their mothers around to handle their dating problems. I'd just have to start pushing for a whole evening of Dave's time and find out where I stood with him.

Chapter Five

Unfortunately I didn't even see Dave for another week, and when I finally did, he was a totally different person from the worried, depressed guy I'd shared pizzas with. It was a Tuesday night, and I was just closing the register when Dave breezed in. "Katie!" His eyes were sparkling, and I could sense a current of excitement about him. "Come have dinner with me tonight. I've got some great news, and I want you to share it."

"Well . . ." I said hesitantly. I wanted to go, but I felt a little angry at Dave, too. I mean, he came by when he felt like it, then I pined away for a whole week waiting for him to come by again. I'd thought an older guy would be more sensitive, but Dave seemed just as wrapped up in himself as any high-school guy. Even more so than many back home.

"Katie, I warn you, I won't take no for an answer. In fact, I'll just wait right here until you're finished, then I'll escort you."

Mr. Tohn looked up from the desk in his office and called, "Are you almost finished, Katie?"

"Listen," Dave whispered, "I don't want to get you in trouble. I'll wait for you outside."

With shaking hands, I finished counting the money as Dave left. He turned and winked before he pushed the door open.

Dave waited right outside the door for me, and as I came out, he grabbed my hand. "Katie, Katie, Katie," he said, laughing happily. "Katie, tell me you'll go out to dinner with me."

"OK, OK." I smiled. "How can I resist someone who's on top of the world. But what are we celebrating?"

"I'll tell you when we get to Pizza Pleasers."

Once inside the restaurant, instead of answering my question, he said, "You know, I was telling someone about you last night, and I discovered how little I knew about you, except that you've saved my sanity this summer. So, Katie, why are you at ASU this summer? What year are you? I don't even know your major or what classes you're trying to get through."

"Well," I said, stalling and trying to figure out a way to change the subject. "Uh, I'm a junior."

Dave laughed. "An older woman. I like that. Now how about your major and your classes this summer?"

Thank goodness the waitress chose that moment to interrupt us. I was trying desperately to think of what to say. How could I tell Dave I was a junior in high school, not in college? Could I pull off a lie and just let him think I was in college? No way! Then I'd have to come up with a major, a class, a professor, and everything else. How could everything be spoiled just when it was starting to be so perfect?

"Uh, it's kind of hard to find out about you when you aren't talking." Dave winked at me, and I realized the waitress had gone and that he was waiting for me to continue.

Well, I thought, *here goes nothing.* Dave wouldn't be interested in me once he knew the truth. Why, oh, why couldn't I have been a couple of years older? I stared at a speck on the table. I wanted to look at Dave, to memorize his face before he was gone, but I was too embarrassed at what I had to tell him. "Dave,"

I said softly, "I'm a junior in high school, not college. I'm just at ASU because my dad is a professor. He's teaching a special economics seminar here this summer."

"Fantastic!" he exclaimed. "I just don't believe it. When my life finally goes right, it really goes right!"

I was totally bewildered. "Dave, what are you talking about?"

He ran his hand through that mass of blond curls, and his intense blue eyes locked into mine. "Katie, I'm so sorry. I must sound completely crazy. I'm just so up, and I've been so down all summer.

"Let me start at the beginning. One of my friend's older brothers owns a ranch up in Colorado, and he invited a bunch of us to come up for part of the summer. All my friends went, including the girl I've been dating, but I had to stay here and go to summer school. You'd think there would be something good about sticking around to do work when everyone else was out having fun, like maybe a great teacher. But who do I get? Old slave driver, Heke, who thinks that a student's waking hours should be spent studying for class.

"The first day I saw you in the drugstore you were so completely into your daydreaming that I was intrigued. I guess I wished I could jump into a daydream, too. Then, when I stopped in again, I'd almost forgotten I'd even met you, but you were so friendly. So on the spur of the moment, I asked you to come to Pizza Pleasers. I was lonely and depressed and needed someone to talk to.

"Then you turned out to be a great listener, and I stopped in to see you again when I needed a second boost. I don't know what I'd have done without having pizza with you those two times. But now everything's changed. For one thing, I aced Heke's midterm. And now all my friends are back. Cindy says she was miserable without me and would have had a better time staying here with me. Isn't that great?"

I fought back the urge to cry. So all I had been was a boost when he was down, someone for him to pass the time with until his real friends and his girlfriend got back into town. Well, one thing was for sure, I wasn't going to let him know how I really felt. At least I could save my pride. Somehow I'd get through that night, and he'd never know how much I cared about him. I put on a phony smile. "Dave, it really is just terrific!"

But things hadn't gotten bad enough yet. He had to make them even worse. "Katie, here is the most incredible part of all. Three days ago my cousin came out to spend the rest of the summer with me. He's a great guy. Whenever I stay with his folks, they always make sure I have a lot of fun. So I want to show him a good time here. But one slight problem. Since my friends are back, I also want to party with them. What I needed to find was a sensitive, good-looking, high-school girl for him to date and bring to our parties. But where? Then presto, my Katie announces she is a high-school junior. Can you believe my luck? Katie, you're just going to love my cousin. Listen, we're having a big swimming party Saturday night. Marc'll pick you up at seven o'clock, and you'll come meet the gang."

Anger and hurt overwhelmed me, but Dave never even noticed. He just babbled on. "I can hardly wait for you to meet Cindy. In fact, it was her idea for me to apologize to you for how cranky I've been during the past few weeks."

I wanted to tell Dave to go away and never come back. Who did he think he was that he could just conveniently give me to his cousin? "Here, Marc, have a soda. Here, Marc, have a date with Katie." If thoughts could kill, Dave would have been a goner. But all I said was,

"Gee, Dave, I can't make it. I already have a date for Saturday night."

He looked like a kid who'd just dropped an ice-cream cone in the sand. I'd spoiled his fun. "Hey, Katie, I'm sorry. I should have asked what was good for you. How about if you tell me what night you can make it, and we'll have the party then."

I was trapped, and I knew it. There was no way to get out of going to the party without Dave's realizing that this little kid, me, had a big crush on him. So I said, "Oh, I guess Friday night would be OK."

Dave leaned across the table and kissed my cheek. "You've got it. A party Friday night for my pretty little Katie."

I couldn't stand any more of Dave's happiness. The evening had gotten quite depressing enough for me, so I said, "Dave, I just couldn't turn you down tonight because you were so excited, but I've got a date in half an hour, and I've really got to get going. I just don't have time to stay and eat."

"Right," said Dave, "I bet you've got tons of dates. My cousin sure is a lucky guy." He told the waitress to keep his pizza warm, and he walked me out the door. That night the air seemed even more like a furnace than usual.

"You know," Dave said, "I don't even know where you live."

I wrote out my address on a piece of paper. It hurt so badly to be that close to Dave and know he didn't care that I couldn't wait to get away from him. "Here." I gave him the piece of paper.

"Great!" he replied happily. "I'll see you Friday night." I started to walk away when he turned me toward him and gave me a big hug. "Katie, thanks for everything. Just wait until everyone meets you."

Chapter Six

This situation was simply too much for me to handle. I needed to talk to Sandy. "Mom," I said quickly once I got home, "I really miss Sandy. Could I call her? Please? I won't stay on the phone very long."

Mom looked at me. I could see in her eyes that she knew things weren't going too well for me. "Go ahead, Katie. Tell Sandy hello for me and don't talk for hours and hours. Oh, and, Katie, if you need another listener, I'm here."

"Thanks, Mom," I called as I headed for the hall phone. I pulled the cord into my room and shut the door.

Sandy answered the phone on the third ring. "Katie! I can't believe it! I miss you so much!"

"I miss you, too, Sandy, but I don't have

much time, and I have a terrible problem. So listen." Quickly I told her what had happened with Dave, and I explained about Marc and the party Friday night. "What am I going to do?" I wailed once the whole awful story was out.

"Let me think for a minute," she said, pausing. "Hmm, Katie, I think I've got it. You're actually going to enjoy that party Friday night. Here's what you've got to do. Work on your tan this week, and on Friday wear your sexiest swimsuit. Don't you see, you've got the perfect chance to make Dave see just how much he *does* care about you. His relationship with Cindy, or whatever her name is, is all in the past. He likes you, I know he does. He just hasn't realized it yet."

"Oh, I really don't—" I began to protest.

"Just listen," Sandy interrupted. "He thought you were pretty enough to find out more about you when he first saw you in the drugstore, and that certainly wasn't when you were looking your best. He's told you several times that he likes your eyes. So just wait until he sees you looking spectacular and all his friends mention how gorgeous you are. Don't give up yet, Katie."

Mom stuck her head in the door and pointed to her watch. I nodded. "Sandy, you're the best friend I could ever have. I've got to hang up, but I'll try your plan. Keep your fingers crossed."

"I will, I will!" she exclaimed. "And be sure to write and tell me every single thing that happens. I bet you'll be sending pictures of you and Dave with the letter!"

I hung up the phone and stared in the mirror. Sandy's plan wasn't going to be all that easy to pull off. It was one thing for her to say that I should look spectacular and another for me to do it. Maybe Dave wouldn't even notice me. Still, it *was* worth a try.

I walked back into the living room where Mom was sitting and knitting. It took some sort of special energy to be working on a wool sweater when it was at least 110 degrees outside. I sat and watched her for a minute or two. She'd tried to show me how to knit lots of times, but I just didn't have the patience for it. "Mom, I've been invited to this party Friday night. . . ."

Mom's hands continued to move as though she hadn't heard me, but I knew she would be interested. I knew my mother thought I was excluding her from my life lately and that she felt badly about it. I guess she was right, but I needed to work some things out by myself right then.

"Anyway, the party is really no big deal.

54

Some guy's younger cousin is in town, and he needs a high schooler to go out with him." The brutal truth of the statement made me feel pretty awful, but I didn't show it. "It's a swimming party, and my old suits are getting a little ragged. So I've decided it would be a good idea to use some of the money I've earned to buy a new suit. Would you come shopping with me?"

Mom put the knitting down. "We haven't been shopping together in ages. Katie, I'd love to go. I'll even take you to lunch first." I had the next day off, so we decided to go then.

In the morning Mom and I woke up early and got to the stores as soon as they opened. Four stores later, we still hadn't found a thing. *Oh, Sandy,* I thought to myself, *your plan may be impossible. I can't even find a passable suit, let alone something spectacular.*

"Katie, you look positively miserable," said Mom. "Come on, cheer up. We'll head for the Tri-City Mall. It's so large, it's bound to have lots of stores that carry swimsuits.

When we got there, Mom insisted we stop for lunch although I really didn't want to. I mean, I had to find something that day, and I didn't think we had time to waste on eating. Besides, in some bathing suits every morsel of food seemed to show up as an unwanted bulge of fat. I ate only a small salad with vinegar and convinced myself that I really wasn't drooling over my mom's cheeseburger.

Finally, we resumed shopping, and as we exhausted all the large department stores in the mall, my sense of desperation grew. "Katie, don't be so down," Mom said. "We'll try some of the smaller stores. You know, it strikes me that finding this suit is pretty important to you. Are you sure you've never even met your date?"

"I'm sure," I said grumpily, "and I am equally sure that I won't like him once I do meet him!" We walked into a small place called Sara's Fashions.

I saw it from the moment we entered the store, the perfect suit. It was a one-piece, green Milliskin with a low-cut back. I could hardly wait to get it off the hanger and try it on. It fit like an absolute dream, as if the suit had been waiting just for me. I stared at myself in the mirror. I felt not only sophisticated, but elegant and sexy as well. What more could anyone ask for?

"Well, Katie," Mom said, "it's beautiful, but it's also double the price of the other suits we've seen. I know you're paying for this with your own money, but I hate to see you spend so much on one thing."

The way I felt was that if the suit helped me get Dave back, it was more than worth the money. Before I could answer my mother, the salesperson walked into the dressing room. "You look stunning!" she exclaimed. "Did you know that there is also a matching cover-up?"

"Oh, I really don't think that we're—" Mom began, but I interrupted her before she could finish and asked the woman to bring it in.

"Mom, it can't hurt just to see it."

As soon as I saw the cover-up, I knew it was totally impractical. It was a short cotton jacket, also green, with capped sleeves. It wouldn't provide much protection from the sun and wouldn't give any warmth on a cool day. I slipped it on, anyway, and glanced in the mirror. I couldn't believe what I saw. I looked absolutely fantastic. It was as if the designer had custom made this outfit just for me.

"I'll take the whole thing," I said firmly to the salesperson, trying not to think of how many hours I'd worked to pay for it.

Mom didn't say anything, but I could tell from her tight-lipped frown that she disapproved. It was my money, and I could spend it however I wished. Still, I knew Mom was disappointed in what she obviously considered a lack of good sense.

I decided that as long as I was splurging I might as well get some new sandals, too. I picked out a pair of white leather thongs trimmed with aqua-colored piping. I also bought a green-and-white beach towel, which I figured would complement the green of the swimsuit. Trying not to think of the dent I'd just made in my school wardrobe fund, I concentrated on how amazed Dave would be when he saw the new Katie. I made a mental note that I'd need new lip gloss and eye shadow to go with the suit.

I spent Thursday and Friday eavesdropping on the conversations of college kids who came into the store, hoping to catch some information on pool parties. But no one said anything of any help. As I was packaging the purchases of one girl, I gathered my courage and ventured, "So, have there been any good pool parties lately?"

She laughed. "Oh, you know how it is. They're all an awful lot alike." I sure wished I did. What a way to experience my first college party. On a blind date with the cousin of the guy I was crazy about.

When I got home from work on Friday afternoon, I rushed to do my hair and take a shower. Mom called to me that a boy named Marc had phoned and said he was looking forward to meeting me. He said he'd pick me up at seven.

Marc. I didn't even like the sound of his name. *Oh, well,* I told myself, *Marc is nothing more than the means to get me to the party tonight.*

Chapter Seven

The doorbell rang while I was still applying a second coat of nail polish. *Well*, I thought, *you can just wait!* Through my closed door, I could hear the vague sounds of conversation and laughter coming from the living room. I waved my hands in the air trying to get my nails to dry faster. I mentally checked to see if I had forgotten any possible bit of preparation for that night. I wished Sandy could have been there to give me a final OK.

Staring at the figure I saw in the mirror, I could hardly believe it was me. The new eye shadow I'd used made my eyes look larger and greener. The swimsuit looked wonderful with a pair of white shorts. I draped the jacket over my shoulder. I felt absolutely elegant. I slipped on my sandals, picked up my new towel and white purse and looked in the mirror once again. Sandy would have been proud!

If only it were Dave out there waiting for me. But then, I'd see him soon enough, and, boy, would he see me!

Marc had been waiting at least fifteen minutes by the time I'd checked every detail of my appearance. I felt kind of bad for my parents having to entertain him for such a long time, but when I walked into the living room, I saw that I needn't have worried. They looked as if they were all in the middle of a great conversation.

"Well, Katie," Dad said, "Marc's great company, but we were wondering if you thought this party was for tomorrow night." Dad hated lateness.

"Oh, that's all right," Marc chimed in. He smiled. It was a friendly smile, but it didn't send shivers up my spine the way Dave's did. "Katie, you are definitely well worth waiting for." I could tell Marc was very impressed with me, and it felt good. In fact, that was exactly the kind of admiring look I wanted to find in Dave's eyes when he saw me that night.

We said goodbye to my folks, and Mom added, "Marc, stop in anytime. It was nice to meet you."

Great, I thought. *Who needs Marc dropping around?*

We began walking to the party. "I hope you don't mind," Marc said. "Dave told me the party was so close to your place that we didn't need a car."

"That's all right," I replied absentmindedly. I was trying to think of exactly what to say to Dave. Should I walk right over to him or casually wait for him to come to me?

Marc kept talking, and I just wished he would be quiet. It was hard to develop a plan and try to listen to Marc's efforts at conversation at the same time. I turned my attention to him briefly. He and Dave certainly didn't look anything alike. Marc's hair was dark brown and straight, and instead of Dave's electrifying blue eyes, Marc's were large and brown like a puppy dog's. He lacked Dave's tan, and while his build was pretty good, he was shorter than Dave by a few inches.

"My cousin Dave said you were really something special," Marc said, smiling, "and he was right."

"Thanks," I replied, but I didn't return the compliment.

He continued to ask me about my job, how I liked Arizona, what I hoped to major in in college. I answered his questions without much thought. It certainly wasn't like being with Dave, when every single word counted.

"Uh, it's right here." Marc opened the gate to a big apartment complex, and I could hear the sounds of the Rolling Stones blaring from a stereo even before I could see about twenty people gathered around the pool. Some kids were sitting talking, some were dancing, and a few were in the pool swimming. All of a sudden I started feeling very nervous. Maybe it would be better to talk to Marc for a little while until I got a feel for the party.

"Let's sit here." I placed myself on a centrally located lounge chair and craned my neck to see just where Dave might be. My hands felt like ice. I squeezed them together, trying to smile at Marc while my eyes continued to search for Dave. Everyone looked so self-assured. Suddenly I wasn't so certain I could carry this whole thing off.

"Looking for anyone special?" asked Marc.

Marc had caught me off guard. "Uh, no, I mean, well actually, I just thought we should tell Dave we're here."

Marc shrugged. "If you want." He stood up and looked around the party. "I don't see him. He mentioned that he and Cindy might go out for dinner. I guess they haven't shown up yet."

"It doesn't really matter," I lied. My mind was racing. *Oh, Sandy,* I thought, *what have I gotten myself into?* It dawned on me that Dave and Cindy might not show up for a couple of hours. By then the heat would have frizzed my hair, and my carefully applied lipstick and eye shadow would surely be smeared. And what was I going to do with Marc? I couldn't just continue to ignore him all night. Nothing was working out right!

Just then the voice I loved to hear called, "Katie, Marc!" and I saw Dave walking toward us.

Quickly I tried to straighten out my cover-up. Panic. Should I stand up? Would I look better if I stayed seated? He was getting closer. I crossed my legs to keep them from shaking and tried to appear casual.

Suddenly Dave was standing right in front of me. I thought I detected a look of admiration in his eyes. He nudged Marc. "Hey, little cousin, I told you she was gorgeous!" I blushed, and Dave continued, "Katie, meet Cindy."

The girl behind Dave smiled at me. Her delicate, elfin face was not at all what I'd expected. She was beautiful, but not in the conventional way I'd imagined. "Katie, it's super to meet you. Thanks for being so great to Dave this summer. I feel terrible about deserting him." Her soft gray eyes turned toward Dave's face, and he put his arm around her. "From now on, I stay right by his side. But thanks again for being so nice."

Dave blushed and looked totally taken by her. "Well," he said, never even looking directly at me or Marc, "you two kids have a great time." Then, eyes still focused on Cindy, he said, "That sounds like a good slow song. Let's dance."

I sat riveted to the spot. How could everything have gone so wrong? I had a crazy impulse to pull Dave back and say, "Wait a minute, you haven't even seen my swimsuit yet, and you can't possibly have noticed my special perfume that was supposed to captivate you when we danced."

Marc sat next to me and put a tentative arm around my shoulders. "I don't blame you for staring. They make a perfect couple. And Cindy is just as nice as she is pretty. I spent about four hours talking to her last night. I really think Dave's picked the perfect girl for himself." Marc smiled and looked at me. "Actually, I'm pretty pleased about my date, too. Can I get you something to eat or drink?"

I tried to answer him, but I felt as if my lips had been glued shut. My throat was on fire, and my eyes burned. "Uhm, maybe something to drink. My throat kind of hurts."

Marc walked off to get me a drink, and I sat still, staring at Dave and Cindy. Their bodies moved as one when they danced, and it was obvious they were totally unaware of anything going on around them.

Carrying two drinks, Marc returned and nodded toward a table. "Let's sit down at that table." My legs felt weak as I stood up, and my whole body was burning hot. I dropped into a seat quickly.

"Katie, you seem kind of flushed. Maybe we should take a swim in the pool. After all," he tried to joke, "we folks from Minnesota just aren't used to living in the middle of an oven."

In some vague part of my brain, it registered that Marc was trying to be very nice to me, but humiliation and hurt had engulfed me so totally that I could barely hear his words. I just wanted the evening to end.

I nodded—not realizing that he had said he was from Minnesota, too—took off my cover-up, and tossed it on the ground.

"Wow! That's a terrific-looking suit," Marc said. We jumped into the pool, and I swam so I wouldn't have to make conversation.

Finally it clicked in my mind that Dave would never even notice if I left. "Marc," I said,

"I don't feel very well. I'm going home. It's just a few blocks, and I can make it fine. You go ahead and stay at the party."

But Marc wouldn't hear of any such thing. He walked me the whole way home, and when we got there, he said, "Katie, it's been great meeting you. I'm sorry you're feeling so awful." He bent slightly, and his lips brushed my forehead. "I'll call you," he whispered as I opened the front door.

I ran to my room and sank into bed, feeling that the best thing for me to do might be to sleep the rest of the summer away.

There was a knock at my door. "Katie," Mom asked, "are you OK?"

"Sure, Mom, I think I'm coming down with a sore throat." She came into my room and put her arm around me. "I'll get you some cough drops, and, Katie, don't worry if tonight didn't work out so well. Sometimes blind dates don't. It really isn't anyone's fault." She brought me the cough drops and said, "Dad and I thought you looked just beautiful tonight."

She shut the door, and in the silent darkness, I put my head in my hands and began to cry.

Chapter Eight

Saturday morning I awoke feeling drained. It was an effort even to brush my teeth. I dressed, not particularly caring what I put on, trudged off to work, and once there, opened the register almost without thinking. Over and over again I asked myself how I could have missed all the signs. Had Dave ever given me any indication that he'd liked me, or had it all been the fantasy of a little girl with a crush?

Mr. Tohn walked over to the register and counted the cash drawer. "Slow morning," he said, frowning. Looking at me pointedly, he said, "You should have plenty of time to start working on your display."

I knew exactly what he meant. I should have completed it by now. Mr. Tohn must be a little disappointed. After all, first I'd bragged what a good design I could produce, and then I'd failed to come up with anything.

"Mr. Tohn," I said, "that display will be done within the next two weeks, and I promise you, it will be good!"

He pushed his glasses back up on the bridge of his nose and looked at me. "Katie, I certainly hope you're right."

After Mr. Tohn walked away, I began sorting through my idea book. There wasn't one really fantastic idea in the whole thing. What was the matter with me? This kind of thing usually came so naturally to me, and stuffed animals should have been easy to display imaginatively. I mean, it wasn't as if I had to do something interesting with a case of aspirin.

I walked over to the stuffed animals and stared at them. It was hard even to see them, all piled into a big bin made of chicken wire. I began to take them out one by one. There was a long pink snake with blue eyes and long eyelashes, a bright green parrot, and among the many teddy bears, one that immediately won my heart: it had a single tear running down its cheek.

The bell on the front door jingled several times, and the store began to fill up with customers. Reluctantly I put the stuffed animals back and returned to the register.

Things stayed unbelievably hectic until closing, and I never got a chance to go back to my stuffed animals, but I had a great idea that I knew would work! I wanted to use the big bay window right in the front of the store. I'd have to convince Mr. Tohn that I knew what I was doing before he'd let me use it, but by Monday I'd be ready with a great sales pitch.

When I got home, I could hardly wait to spread out my sketchbook and put down on paper everything that was so clear in my mind. I was in a great mood until Mom called out, "Katie, is that you? Marc's called you twice today. When he missed you the second time, he said he was glad you felt better and since you had a date tonight, he'd call you tomorrow." Mom walked into the living room looking a little perplexed. "Do you have a date tonight?"

"Well, uh—" I stammered, "not really. I just sort of said that to a guy named Dave, and I guess he told Marc."

"Oh," said Mom. She ran a hand through her short red hair and looked at Dad, who was sitting in his chair fidgeting with his pipe.

My father took a deep puff. "I like that Marc. He seemed like a very nice young man."

"Uh-huh," I replied. "Guess what! I've got the best idea for my display. I can hardly wait to sketch it for you."

"Great, Katie," Mom said. "We really want to see it. But can it possibly wait for a little bit? It's so hot that I thought we'd go out for dinner instead of cooking. What do you think about pizza?"

I winced a little. Pizza again, but this time without Dave sitting across from me. Then I thought of something terrible. What if I ran into Dave and his friends and I was out on a Saturday night with my parents? "Let's drive into Phoenix," I ventured. "We can make a whole night of it."

To my surprise Mom and Dad agreed. Though I didn't really feel like leaving my designing for the entire evening, it was better than having Dave see that my "date" was my parents. As we walked out of the house and headed toward the car, Dad caught and held Mom's hand. I decided, that as parents went, they were pretty special people.

When we got home, it was late, and I was too tired to draw. As I got ready for bed, Mom knocked on my door. "Katie, I completely forgot. This came for you in the mail today." She handed me an envelope.

It was a letter from Sandy. She must have

written it right after we'd talked on the phone because she babbled on about the wonderful time I was going to have at the party.

Dear Katie,

I only wish I could see you Friday night. I know you're going to look smashing! That Cindy will never even have a chance! I know that by the time you get this the big evening will be over, but I have such a strong feeling that everything will turn out great. I had this dream a couple of days ago, even before you ever called. It was homecoming, and you were there with some guy. I couldn't see his face, but all the girls were so impressed because he'd come from another city just to be with you. Anyway, now I know it must have been Dave. I must have ESP!

I've been seeing Kenny pretty regularly. He's nice, and we do have fun together. If things keep going this way, I may even skip some of our Friday night sleep-overs for dates! Maybe we're finally growing up, and we won't have to spend all our time playing what-if games. One thing is for sure, even if we don't spend as much time together, you'll always be my best friend.

Well, this letter has gone on and on, and I've got writer's cramp, so I'll end, but I just bet I'll get that picture of Dave with his arm around you real soon.

Love,
Sandy

I folded the letter and put it down. I didn't think anything could have made me feel worse about Friday night than I already felt, but somehow, Sandy's letter had done just that.

Chapter Nine

Sunday morning started with the jarring ring of the telephone. *Boy*, I thought groggily as I walked out into the hall and picked up the phone, *whoever's calling can't know us very well*. I focused bleary-eyed on my clock radio as I crossed back into my room. It was only nine. No one in our house ever got up before ten on Sundays.

"Hello?" I answered sleepily.

"Katie?" questioned a deep male voice on the other end of the phone.

My eyes flew open. I was instantly wide-awake. "Who's calling?" I asked stalling.

"Uh, this is Marc, Marc Cook."

I hesitated a second, then I spoke. "This is Mrs. Thompson. I'm afraid Katie has left for

74

the day. She went on a picnic with some friends."

"Thanks, anyway," Marc said, and I could hear the disappointment in his voice.

I replaced the receiver with a twinge of guilt. I tried to picture Marc in my mind, but I couldn't see his face. All I could think of was Dave, his arm wrapped around Cindy, smugly advising us little kids to go have a good time. Boy, just who did Dave think he was, anyway?

I was really wide-awake now, so I took out my sketchbook and began to draw. It was all so easy. The animals had inspired the whole thing for me. All I'd had to do was to look at them. I'd create a jungle scene. The monkeys could hang from a tree. The frog would sit on a pond of tinfoil. The parrot, the zebra, the snake, and even my teddy bear with a tear would fit in perfectly. The scene would be colorful and eye-catching. As some animals were sold, I could replace them with others, and the jungle would be constantly changing. I drew the scene as best I could, painted it carefully, and hoped that Mr. Tohn would give it his OK. It just had to go in the front window.

Monday morning when Mr. Tohn got to the store, I was already waiting for him at the door. He looked at me quizzically. "Set your alarm too early this morning?"

"Mr. Tohn," I exclaimed, "I've designed your display, and it's going to be out-standing!"

"Well, at least let me get the door open first. I'm not sure this old man can take so much enthusiasm before eight-thirty in the morning." He stuck his key in the alarm and then in the lock. "Let's go in."

I followed meekly behind him as he led the way to his office. "Mr. Tohn, this display just has to go in the front bay window. It will fit perfectly."

He opened his old-fashioned rolltop desk and motioned me to a chair beside it. "Well," he said sternly, "let's see what you've got. I told you you could do the display. I did not say that you could have my prime bay window for it."

"I know, I know. I'll understand if you say no, but I think you're going to love it!"

I took out the drawing. Mr. Tohn looked at it, adjusted his glasses, and looked again. "You're quite an artist. This is remarkable." Then he quickly checked himself. "Katie, I told you I'd give you twenty dollars for supplies. I don't see how you could do this for much under two hundred. I'm afraid it's out of the question."

"Please, Mr. Tohn," I begged. "It won't cost that much. I know it won't. I've bought lots of art supplies for projects, and it never costs that much."

"Well—I suppose we could go look at the window."

It was a perfect, old-fashioned bay window, ideally suited for the somewhat old-fashioned store. There was a picket fence to keep people from walking right into the display area. I'd have to do something about that fence. It certainly didn't belong in a jungle.

Anyone who had wandered in the store at that moment would have seen an older, balding man and a teenage girl, both standing before a bay window, each totally absorbed in thought. Finally Mr. Tohn broke the silence. "You know, when we first built this store, my wife insisted on the window." He chuckled. "She said, 'Jim, I'll leave Maine and follow you out to the Arizona desert. I'll move into a small apartment and help in the store. But if we can't afford a New England house, we'll at least have to build a proper bay window in the store."

Mr. Tohn continued, but I knew he'd forgotten I was even there. His eyes had a faraway look in them as he remembered times long past. "So we built the store with the biggest darn bay window the place could handle. All around us, neighbors with stucco and tile buildings shook their heads and whispered behind our backs that we stood out like a sore thumb. But when the window was finished, Martha said it was perfect. That must have been twenty, no, by gosh, it was thirty years ago. How fast time passes."

His eyes were misted. Then, as if he'd suddenly become aware that I was standing there, he coughed. "OK, Miss Katie Thompson. This window"—he ran his finger along a dust-covered box of Anacin—"could use some updating. I'll cover your expenses up to twenty dollars, but not one penny more."

"Oh, thank you. Thank you!" I felt like hugging him. "You'll see, Mr. Tohn, I'll make it a window you and your wife will be proud of."

"You do that," he said quietly, and then he was lost again in memories.

I walked over to the register, my heart pounding with excitement. Who'd ever have thought Mr. Tohn had such romantic memories of his wife? The lights went on, and I heard Mr. Tohn turn the sign on the door from "closed" to "open." Another day at University Drugs had begun.

I decided that the only intelligent way to approach the display project was to make a list of every type of stuffed animal we had and keep track of the number of each. That way I'd know which ones to put in the display. Besides, that was the only thing I could do while at work, and I didn't dare ask Mr. Tohn for time off to go get supplies.

I kept staring at that little three-foot picket fence. If I just took it away, people might step right into the window. Besides, it seemed to be pretty thoroughly nailed into the floor. I'd just have to cover it with something. But what?

Four girls walked up to the register with some dye. "Do you know anything about over-dyeing?" they asked.

"Gosh, I'm sorry, but I don't. It sure is popular, though. I walked by a fabric store in the Tri-City Mall the other day, and they had tons of overdyed material."

"Well, we're experimenting with some sorority jean jackets," said a tall girl with long black hair that reached almost to her waist, "and we really aren't sure what we're doing."

"Good luck!" I said as I handed them their change. "Stop in and model them when you're finished."

"Oh, we sure will," replied one girl.

Another added, "That is, if we're fit to be seen outside the sorority house in the finished product."

I watched them leave, thinking that maybe they'd be better off buying the material already overdyed. It had been in the fabric store right next to an awful forest print that Mom and I had laughed about. *That's it!* I thought excitedly. *It would be just perfect for my display—I could use it to cover the picket fence.* I could hardly wait to go back and get it. I wished I'd paid more attention to the price; I hoped that it wouldn't be too expensive.

If only Sandy were here now, I thought, *or for that matter, anyone I knew. It would be so great to be able to talk to someone about all this.* Almost as if he'd heard my thoughts, a familiar male figure approached the register, his brown hair falling in his eyes. In his hand he carried a long-stemmed red rose. He looked a little nervous, and in his eyes I could sense a certain weariness.

"Hi, Katie."

"Well, hi, Marc!" I responded warmly. "I'm glad you stopped in." And I was. I was ready to shout my plan about the jungle to the whole world. At least I knew Marc a little, and somehow, I had the feeling that he'd really be interested.

He smiled. "I'm glad you're glad to see me. I brought you something." He thrust the rose

80

toward me. "I've been trying to get hold of you. Aren't you ever home?"

I feigned innocence. "I'm sorry you missed me before," I said, feeling kind of like a rat. "Anyway, I'm happy to see you now. I've got this great project I've started here. Let me tell you about it."

"I'd love to hear," he replied, and I could tell that he meant it. I decided that Marc wasn't such a bad guy. There was something warm and kind and reassuring about him. Maybe we could be friends. We just wouldn't discuss Dave. "Hey, listen," he continued, "Dave said you really like Pizza Pleasers. Why don't I take you there after work, and we'll celebrate your project?"

Something in me started to freeze at the mere mention of Dave's name, and Marc bumbled on making things worse. "You know, I couldn't quite decide if you were really sick the other night or just sick of your date. When I kept calling and you were never home, I decided that you were avoiding me. But Dave insisted that I was being paranoid. He said he knew you well enough to know we'd be a great couple, and he said I should get over here and straighten things out soon enough for us to double with him and Cindy to the jazz concert next weekend."

Inside, I was exploding with rage. Dave would not control me like I was some little puppy dog available to keep his cousin occupied. It could only have been the excitement of the display that had allowed me to drop my guard. It wouldn't happen again. I could never consider double-dating and watching Dave adore Cindy all night.

"Listen, Marc," I said choosing my words carefully since I was sure they'd be repeated to Dave, "I'm glad you stopped in, and the rose is really pretty, but you see I usually date older guys. I have nothing against you personally, you understand." I couldn't resist adding, "Marc, I'm sorry, but I guess Dave doesn't really know me very well after all."

"I understand," he said abruptly. "Well, it wasn't a total loss. This little high-school boy left you with a rose, at least. Bye, Katie, thanks for the conversation." Marc turned on his heel and marched out the door.

With a tinge of regret, I watched him go. I'd just cut myself off from the only person who'd really been interested in me since I got to ASU. Well, it was done, and I was better off without any more contact with Dave or any of his friends or relatives. The heaviness in the pit of my stomach would disappear eventually.

Chapter Ten

The next few days were such a blur of activity that I didn't have time to think of Dave or Marc or anyone. It started when I'd gotten home from work that day and told Mom and Dad all about my plans for the window.

Dad beamed. "Well, that's my princess. Next year I'll get invited back because Mr. Tohn will want my daughter's display expertise."

I was glad he and Mom were so enthusiastic. Mom even offered to run me back to the Tri-City Mall to get my material. "We can't take a chance on someone else's buying it," she said.

Luck was going my way. Not only was the fabric still there, but it had been reduced from three dollars a yard to just seventy-nine

83

cents. I parted with seven dollars and ninety cents and left the store with ten yards of kelly green fabric with bamboo shoots, exotic leaves, and birds floating across it.

On the way home I told Mom I wished I could use a real mirror instead of foil for my jungle pond, but I was afraid that it would kill my budget entirely.

"Katie," exclaimed Mom, "I've got a great idea! Mrs. Miller—she lives three doors down—was just telling me about a second-hand store that has all sorts of unusual things. It's too late tonight, but we could try it on your day off."

"That would be great," I said, crossing my fingers and hoping that the place might some-how have a cheap round or oval mirror. We pulled into our parking place and walked into the house.

"Well, it's about time the two of you got back," thundered Dad. We really hadn't been gone very long, and I couldn't figure out why he sounded so upset. But then I saw the twin-kling in his eyes. "You two think you're the only ones who can get involved in creating this jungle?" He swept his hand through the air with a majestic flourish. "I have found trees!" I know my mouth dropped open, and I'm sure

Mom's must have, too. "Well," continued Dad, "don't you even want to know what I mean?"

"Yes, yes, of course," Mom said, laughing.

"Tell us, tell us!" I begged.

"Well, that's more the excitement I had in mind," said Dad, and he explained that after we'd left, he'd begun wondering what he could do to help. Then he'd remembered a lunchtime conversation he'd had in the faculty dining room with Charles Schmidt, head of the theater department. Mr. Schmidt had been talking about tearing apart and tossing out some old sets. "So, tonight I called him and asked him if, by any chance, those old props included any bushes or trees. When he said yes, I asked him to hold on to them until tomorrow and that we'd take them off his hands. He was delighted and said we would save his technical crew from having to break them up and cart them away. But he wants them out immediately. So, see if Mr. Tohn can spare you for just an hour tomorrow. If he can I'll meet you after my two-forty class, and we'll figure out a way to get the forest to the drugstore."

I ran over to Dad and hugged him tightly. To most of the world he was a great economics theoretician and professor, but to me he was the best father I could ever dream of.

The next morning I could hardly wait to get to work. "Mr. Tohn, Mr. Tohn," I called breathlessly as I tried the locked door. I could see the light in the office.

He came to the door, unlocked it, and let me in. "Katie," he said looking at his watch, "it's only eight in the morning. What on earth are you doing here? And how did you ever know I'd be in this early?"

"I didn't know, but I had to give it a try." My words tumbled out one after another as I rushed to tell Mr. Tohn everything.

"Katie, I have been in the business for a long, long time, and I've probably had hundreds of kids cashier for me. I've heard most of the excuses in the world for coming in late or getting off early, but I've never had anyone ask me for an hour off in the middle of the day to get trees. Just who do you think is going to cover the register while you're gone?"

I looked at the floor, drew on all my courage, and in a very small voice said, "Uh, could you?"

Mr. Tohn's eyes widened as if he couldn't quite believe the whole situation. Then he started to smile, but quickly stopped himself. "This will not ever happen again, so don't even consider asking, no matter what the reason.

You'll have precisely one hour today and no more. Is that clearly understood, young lady?"

I assured him it was and thanked him again and again. "As long as I'm already here, do you mind if I start cleaning out the window, or is there something else I can do to make up for not being here this afternoon?"

"Oh, go work on your window and let me get my work done in peace! I have to hurry so that I can take over for my counter girl this afternoon!" In spite of his words, I could sense that Mr. Tohn was kind of excited about the project, too. I knew I'd better produce something good.

I called the secretary at the economics department and left a message for Dad saying that I'd meet him at three-thirty outside his classroom. Then I went to work on the window. Taking a roll of paper towels from the restroom, I started to ask Mr. Tohn what he wanted done with the old cardboard cutouts currently in the window, but seeing him concentrating on his work, I decided not to press my luck by interrupting him again. I could just stack everything by the back door and ask him later. As I took the cutouts from the window, I wondered how long they had been there. The colors were so sun faded that I could hardly tell what colors they had been originally. The window floor was filthy. The roll of paper towels was used up in nothing flat, and the windowsill needed a lot of cleaning.

Almost before I knew it, it was a quarter to nine. I looked at myself. My hands were filthy, my skirt was rumpled, and there were some grayish spots on my white blouse. I could only imagine what my hair and face must look like. I went to the restroom and cleaned myself up the best I could. Staring in the mirror, I had to laugh at the image that greeted me. With my dirt-smudged nose, I looked a lot like a little kid who'd been out playing in the mud.

All morning I kept glancing at the window. Three-thirty couldn't come fast enough for me, and when it finally arrived, I tried hard not to be impatient when Mr. Tohn had to attend to one detail after another. After all, the counter girl couldn't very well order her boss to take over her register. Finally Mr. Tohn came over to the register. "Remember, Katie, no more than one hour!"

I flew out the door and to the campus. In spite of my resolution to explore the campus, I'd barely set foot on it, and I still hadn't gone to one of Dad's classes. Since I didn't know my way around, I had to keep stopping people to ask for directions to the business building.

I walked by the outdoor courtyard of the Student Union, thinking how pretty it was. I did some people-watching as I walked. Suddenly I caught sight of a familiar face. It was Marc, and he was holding hands with a pretty, red-haired girl. The two of them seemed absorbed in conversation, and neither saw me pass by.

Well, I thought to myself, *it certainly didn't take him long to get over me.* I stared at him and the girl a minute more and felt a stab of something strange. Could it be jealousy? *Of course not!* I told myself. *After all, it's Dave I like.* Then why did I have a crazy urge to run back, tell Marc about my whole display project, and invite him to come with me to help set it up? I was probably just suffering from a combination of too little sleep and too much excitement.

As I headed for the business building, I wasn't quite so excited as I had been, and I couldn't resist turning and looking back at Marc and the girl once more.

Chapter Eleven

The storage room of the theater department was the most incredible place. Charles Schmidt led Dad and me to three trees and four bushes. "I hope you can use some of these. They're a little the worse for wear and not as realistic as they might be," he apologized.

They were a million times better than anything we'd ever made in high school and certainly far better than what I'd planned to create myself. I wanted to take them all, but I knew no more than one bush and a couple of trees could fit in the window. Dad and I loaded them into the backseat of the car. Thank goodness it had a sunroof. We stood the trees upright and stuck them through the roof.

Mr. Schmidt followed us to the car, and I

thanked him again and again. "Well," he said, smiling and looking at the sight of the trees sticking out of the roof of the car, "I'm glad I could help. I may have to drop by and see the finished project."

More than a few heads turned as we drove through campus and pulled up at University Drugs. Mr. Tohn came out and shook Dad's hand. "Need some help?" he inquired, looking rather amazed at the forest-filled car. He and Dad stood making small talk. Mr. Tohn looked at me. "Someone," he said pointedly, "should be taking care of the register."

As I started into the store, I overheard Mr. Tohn laughingly tell my dad that he had quite a daughter. They seemed to talk forever, and they moved into the shade to escape the heat. I knew that the intense sun couldn't be doing my forest any good, but I was afraid to interrupt them. I concentrated hard trying to will them to bring in my bush and trees.

Perhaps that's why I didn't notice the two figures who were watching me. "Well, some things never change," said a voice, which sounded slightly sarcastic. I looked up. Dave had caught me daydreaming once again.

I blushed in spite of myself, thinking how disheveled I must be. Between cleaning the window and getting the bushes, I didn't need a mirror to know that I was looking far from my best.

Cindy, her arm linked with Dave's, ended the awkwardness of our silence. "Katie, it's good to see you again. This looks like a fun job."

"Oh, it is," I replied. "Right now I'm working on this display. That's why I'm a little dirty, but it's—"

"Darn! I forgot shaving cream," Dave interrupted almost as if talking to himself. He and Cindy disengaged themselves, and he went back for it.

Cindy leaned toward me. "Don't pay any attention to him. If Dave seems a little weird, it's just because he was so sure that his matchmaking would work out. He doesn't like to be wrong. But don't worry about Marc, he's not your responsibility. Besides, I've introduced him to a couple of freshmen girls who seem to like him a lot."

"I'm glad," I said. I smiled brightly at Cindy, but somehow her statement about Marc made me feel worse instead of better. Dave returned, and I rang up his shaving cream and the other items he'd laid on the counter.

"Well," Cindy said, "take care. We'll probably be seeing you around."

"Right—anytime you stop in University Drugs," I said.

I watched Dave and Cindy leave and then focused on Dad and Mr. Tohn who were still talking. Finally, just as I was about to go out to them, they began bringing in the greenery. There was no place to put the trees and still keep them out of the way except in Mr. Tohn's office.

"I don't know, Jim," Dad said. "You hire my daughter and in a matter of weeks she tears apart your front window and turns your office into a forest with no room for people. You'd better watch out. She could be dangerous." Mr. Tohn actually laughed.

Once the trees were taken care of, Dad came over, kissed me on the top of my head, and left. It was only an hour until closing, and I was relieved that the day was almost over. All the hurrying and the morning's early start had taken their toll. I was exhausted.

I closed the register and went back to Mr. Tohn's office. He looked distinctly displeased as he peered up from his desk from among the trees and bushes. "Well, Miss Thompson, I do hope these will find their way out of here very soon."

"Oh, they will. I just want to stare at them a few minutes more to fix them in my mind before I leave." Mr. Tohn shook his head and went back to his accounting. There was something sort of funny about the way his balding head peeked out from all that greenery, but I knew better than to laugh.

I stared hard at the scenery. Made of crepe paper, chicken wire, wood, canvas, and paint, the trees and bushes looked perfect for my fantasy jungle. When I was sure I could reproduce them in sketches, I tiptoed out of the office, careful not to disturb Mr. Tohn any further.

Out on the street the heat seemed even more intense than usual. Maybe that was because I'd already been out in it twice that day. I willed myself not to think about it, to concentrate on something else. Then I remembered I'd jammed some newspaper articles in my purse that Sandy had sent with her letter. I was so depressed about the letter that I'd never read the articles. I pulled them from my purse and began to look them over. Engrossed in my reading, I let my feet carry me toward home almost without thinking.

All of a sudden my arm and shoulder connected with something. I looked up from the articles, startled. Staring back at me, and looking none too pleased, was Marc. "I—"

"Don't bother," interrupted Marc. "I really

don't need another brush-off. I certainly didn't plan this. In fact, it was you who smacked into me. So you just keep walking your way, I'll keep walking mine, and we'll forget we ever saw each other."

Though I was shocked by the force of his words, it was the look in his eyes that hit me. Those warm, soft brown eyes revealed anger, humiliation, and hurt. I recognized those feelings all too well. I'd felt them myself.

Marc strode angrily away. I stood riveted to the spot, realizing how I must have seemed to Marc. I was no better than Dave. The only person I'd thought about was myself. What had Marc ever done except try to be kind and attentive? I'd wanted sensitivity in a guy, and I'd thought I'd found that quality in Dave. Well, he sure didn't have it, but Marc did! And I'd ignored him selfishly to get back at Dave.

"Marc," I turned and shouted to the quickly disappearing figure. "Marc!" He either didn't hear me or was ignoring me because he wasn't stopping. I cupped my hands to my mouth and yelled as loudly as I could, "Marc, please wait!"

Several people stared at me, but I didn't care. Marc stopped and turned toward me, looking puzzled.

"Please, wait a minute," I called. He stood

right where he had stopped. It was obvious that he wasn't coming any closer, but at least he wasn't walking away.

My cheeks were on fire, and I was feeling dizzy. I'd just apologize to Marc, and then I'd get straight home. He probably didn't care what I had to say, but it was important for me, at least, to say it. My feet felt heavy, but finally I was standing in front of him. His eyes didn't mask his confusion or the fact that he was on guard.

"Marc," I said, "I—" The world began to blur. "I think I'm going to pass out." My voice sounded very far away, and I felt a strong arm around my shoulders. It guided me inside a restaurant and sat me down. The air-conditioning did me a lot of good, and the black and red spots in front of my eyes began to clear. I saw Marc bringing some wet napkins toward me.

"Here, put these on your forehead, they'll help you cool off. Are you OK?" There was real concern in his voice. I was so ashamed of the way I'd acted toward Marc that, to my horror, I began to cry. "Listen," Marc said, putting his arm around me, "can I call your folks for you? Katie, whatever it is, I'll try to help you, and then I promise, you'll never have to see me again. Just don't cry. Look, can I buy you something cold to drink?"

My head was clear enough to realize we were in a small restaurant, and I nodded yes as I tried to regain my composure. "Really, Marc, I'm OK. I think I just got a little too much heat and sun. I had a long day today, and I guess I forgot to eat." I shrugged, feeling totally stupid. "Everything just caught up with me at once."

Sensing I was OK, Marc put on a careful mask of indifference again. I had an urge to reach out and take his hand, but I didn't. I just began to speak. I wasn't sure what I was going to say, I just hoped that somehow I'd find the right words. "Marc, I didn't call to you because I felt sick. I wouldn't blame you if you didn't believe me. I know I've acted terribly." I took a deep breath. "I asked you to wait for me because—because I wanted to apologize to you."

"I'm a big boy, no apologies are necessary. Even my presence seems to make you sick."

Oh, boy, I thought, *he's definitely not going to make this easy on me.* Then I did take his hand. I held it firmly, as if I could make him believe me by holding it.

"But, Marc, apologies are necessary. I was awful to you, and it honestly had nothing to do with anything you said or did." I chose my words carefully. "I was very upset about something else, and I took it out on you. I wouldn't blame you if you never wanted to see me again. But I want you to know that I'm truly sorry for the way I acted." Then I blurted out, "And I want you to know what a really nice person I think you are." An embarrassed silence loomed between us. Finally I said, "Listen, I don't think I need that cold drink. I'm feeling well enough now to walk home. Thanks for the rescue."

I started to get up. "Wait a minute," Marc commanded. "You'd better get something in your stomach before you leave. After all," he added, "friends have to watch out for each other."

"Thanks." I smiled and sat back down. We ordered root-beer floats, and the cold drink and sweet ice cream were instantly reviving.

"How come you're so worn out today?" Marc asked. He seemed so interested that it wasn't long before I was telling him all about my display and why it meant so much to me. I told him about the trees and bushes and about my hope for a mirror for the pond. "I really wish I could get hold of some of that artificial grass they use on football fields, but the stuff costs way too much for my budget."

Marc was such a good listener that we talked for almost an hour before I realized how much time had passed. "Gosh," I said, "I'd better get home. Want to come with me?" Then remembering what Cindy had said earlier about Marc meeting a couple of girls who liked him, I added, "That is if you're not already busy."

"I'll walk you home," he said firmly. "After all, we can't have you passing out on some stranger every couple of blocks." He smiled, and my heart fluttered. His smile had its own special charm.

Walking toward my house, I began to ask Marc about himself, realizing how little I knew. "Well, let's see," he said teasingly, "a two-minute biography of Marc Cook. I am going to be a senior at New Heights High in Duluth, Minnesota. I broke my nose twice playing football there." He touched a slightly crooked spot. "And then I decided I'd had enough pain, and I quit. This fall I'll be the chairman of the school homecoming week, which some people call an honor and others call insane. I have two little sisters, two parents, and a dog named Zingo. I hope to go to college at ASU, which is one reason I came to see Dave this summer. I plan to major in business, and someday you'll see M. Cook's

Sporting Goods stores all over the state of Minnesota, and you can say you knew me when. How's that for a quick but thorough summary of my life?"

I was having such a nice time walking and talking with Marc that we reached my house all too soon. "Why don't you come in and have a bite to eat? After all," I said lightly, "I can't have you weak from hunger and passing out on every girl along the way home."

He laughed. "Oh, I don't know, that might be kind of fun." Then he turned serious. "I'd love to come in, but I've got a—" He looked at the ground. "I've got some plans for tonight. But, Katie, I'm glad we're friends."

"Well," I said, masking a sudden sense of disappointment, "maybe you'll stop by the store to see my display soon."

"I'll sure try. Katie, I've really got to go," he said, looking at his watch. "I'm glad we ran into each other." He laughed, waved, and walked away.

I went inside, and then, impulsively, I peeked out through the curtains to watch him go. *So*, I thought, *Marc has a date tonight. That's what he was about to say.* I wondered if it was with the girl I'd seen him talking to earlier in the day. I sighed and closed the curtains. Why couldn't life ever be simple?

Chapter Twelve

The house was empty, but there was a note on the kitchen table that read, "Katie, good news! I got the job in Minnesota as personnel manager with Levinton and Sons. I went to show your father the letter. If we're not back by six, we went out to eat. There's tuna in the refrigerator if you're hungry. Hope all went well with your trees. Love, Mom."

Having an interview for that job was just about the last thing Mom had done before we'd come to Arizona. She'd been as scared as I'd ever been for any big exam. I knew how badly she wanted the job. It was absolutely terrific that she'd gotten it. I could hardly wait to hear all the details.

The root-beer float I'd had with Marc dulled my appetite enough so that I didn't feel like the tuna. Instead, I took a cool shower, washed my hair, and flopped in the big easy chair in the living room. The air-conditioning blew through my wet hair, and I actually felt chilled, a wonderful feeling on that hot summer day.

After switching the channels, I decided there was really nothing on TV and turned it off. Silence hung heavily in the air. Tilting my head against the vinyl of the chair, I drifted off to a dream-filled sleep. Suddenly I was in the jungle I'd created. Only it was huge, and I was lost. The animals had all come alive, and though I kept trying to tell the snake that real animals weren't pink, it just hissed, "Silly girl." I asked the teddy bear with the tear why he cried, but he simply shook his head mutely. "Can I brush your tear away?" I reached out to touch him, and he disappeared. Far off in the distance, I saw Dave, Cindy, Marc, and a few other kids having a picnic. I called to them, but a big piece of glass separated us, and they couldn't hear me.

I guess I was still calling, "Hello, hello," in my sleep when I felt a hand on my shoulder. My eyes flew open, and I saw my dad standing in front of me. "Are you OK?"

"Yeah, I'm fine. I fell asleep, and I guess I was sort of having a nightmare." I rubbed my eyes, thinking what a strange dream it had been. It hadn't made any sense. Or had it?

Mom came into the living room. "Katie, I'm sorry I didn't wait for you. I was just so excited."

"Mom," I cried enthusiastically, "I'm so proud of you. Tell me about the letter."

She explained that not only had she been offered the position, but the company had also agreed to hold the job open for her until she returned to Minneapolis at the end of the summer. "You know," she said, "the day I got my master's degree in business, I wondered why I'd done it. I figured no one was ever going to hire someone my age. I almost didn't even sign up for job interviews. But the morning I went for my interview with Levinton and Sons, I realized just how much I really wanted the job. I was afraid even to think about it, and then when I didn't hear anything—well, I just assumed they'd hired someone else."

"I'm so proud of both of you," said Dad, "for having the courage to go after what you really want to do!"

"Oh, Katie, your trees! What does your forest look like?" Mom asked. "In all the excitement, I almost forgot to ask."

I went into great detail about everything, and then Mom apologized again. "I know we always share things, but I was so excited I just couldn't wait. Forgive me?"

"Sure," I said, and then I added casually, "I wasn't really all that lonely. I ran into Marc on the way home, and he walked me here."

"You should have asked him to stay," Mom said. I decided I'd better change the topic before my parents started asking questions I didn't want to answer, so I steered the conversation back to Mom's new job.

Chapter Thirteen

On Wednesday, my day off, I was up and dressed by nine and ready to go to the little secondhand store Mom had said might have a cheap mirror. Mrs. Miller hadn't remembered the address or the exact name, and just as Mom and I decided we'd never find the place, we saw an old adobe house with a handcrafted wooden sign that read: Rosie's Secondhand Items—Used But Never Abused.

"Oh my," exclaimed Mom as we walked inside. There seemed to be no particular order to anything, but every available foot of space was used. Clothes were packed so tightly on racks that it was almost impossible to yank out a single item. An old lamp lay in a baby carriage, a feather duster stuck out of a large plastic Christmas tree as an odd branch, and a jewelry display sat atop a used microwave oven.

"Can I help you?" bellowed a rotund lady in a shapeless gray dress.

"What an incredible place you have!" I recognized that tone in Mom's voice. It meant "I'm fascinated, and I plan to stay awhile." Normally I'd have joined in her sense of adventure, but that day I just wanted to get my mirror and get back to work.

The woman, obviously Rosie, walked over to Mom. "I'm so glad you like it here. Some folks think it's all a bunch of junk, but I say beauty is in the eye of the beholder."

"Do you have a piece of mirror?" I asked rather timidly.

"Mirror? I'm sure I saw some around here a few weeks ago. I'll just have to look. It's hard to know just what's buried where."

I tried to wait patiently while she plowed through the store. "Ah ha, I found them!" she said with satisfaction. "Do you want a round mirror that's just a little warped, or do you want a long mirror that's just a little crooked?" She held them up. The round mirror was perfect for my pond.

"That one," I said and pointed. "How much do you want for that one?"

We settled on four dollars, and I put the mirror into the car. Finally I dragged Mom away. As we left the sun glinted off the mirror, casting strange patterns of light. I looked back at the strange little store, and I felt as if I were stepping out of a Mary Poppins adventure.

Arriving at the drugstore, Mom and I each took an end of the mirror and carried it in the store, past the guy who worked as cashier on my day off, and into Mr. Tohn's office. His eyes about popped out of his head. It's a good thing Mom was standing there, or I'm not sure what he'd have said. "I promise, Mr. Tohn, this stuff will all be out of here by tomorrow night. I'll work on the window all day today."

Mr. Tohn just shook his head and muttered, "Thank heavens I didn't tell her she could remodel the prescription department!"

I was dressed in cutoffs and a T-shirt, and I was afraid Mr. Tohn wouldn't be too happy about that, but at least I wouldn't be waiting on any customers.

Mom left, and after I introduced myself to the guy behind the cash register—I had never been in on my day off before—I went to a pay phone to make some calls about artificial grass. I didn't think Mr. Tohn would appreciate my using his phone. As I made the first call, I crossed my fingers. Everything else was working out so well that maybe the Astroturf would be cheaper than I thought. Five phone calls later I found out that the artificial grass would cost more than double my entire budget. There was no way I could swing it. I'd just have to paint pieces of cardboard green and lay them in as grass. Disappointed, I headed down the street to the art store for cardboard and green paint. Five more dollars slipped easily away.

I took all my purchases around to the alley behind the drugstore, figuring that in the heat the paint would dry within a half hour. Finishing quickly, I looked at my work critically. I was in big trouble if it still looked that bad when it was dry.

Since I had to wait anyway, I ran down to Pizza Pleasers for a soda. *Funny,* I thought, *it doesn't bother me to be here anymore.* Pizza Pleasers no longer seemed romantic or painful, it was just a place where I could get a cold drink. The root beer tasted delicious as it slid down my parched throat. As I drank, I had to chuckle at myself. There were specks of green paint all over my arms, and I figured they were on my face and in my hair, too.

When I went back to the alley, the paint was dry. Unfortunately the cardboard looked no better, but it was all I had to work with. Carrying the large panels into the store, I saw Mr. Tohn cover his eyes with his hands and look away. At least I took the cardboard right to the window. That was where it belonged for the display, and besides, nothing more would fit in Mr. Tohn's office.

I laid the cardboard down until the entire window floor was green. Then I began to cart the two trees out. Standing back to survey what I'd done so far, I fought a wave of disappointment. The trees hadn't been able to hide the pathetic cardboard grass. I hoped the whole window wouldn't end up looking like a fifth-grade art project.

A hand tapped me on the shoulder, and I jumped and turned, expecting to see Mr. Tohn. "You the one who is supposed to get this artificial grass?"

"Marc," I gasped. "What are you doing here? What are you talking about?"

He motioned to the truck behind him. "It's double-parked. It belongs to a friend of Dave's, and he'll be plenty mad if I get a ticket. So if you want the artificial grass I've got in the back, I'd better get it out fast."

I stood speechless, and as he started to walk away, I called, "Wait, I don't understand—" but Marc was out the door.

When I caught up with him, he was hoisting a big roll of Astroturf onto his shoulder. He carried it to the sidewalk and dumped it on the ground. "Be back in a sec," he said as he hopped into the truck.

I unrolled the material a little. It was perfect. But how and where had Marc ever found it? I tried to move the roll into the store but discovered it was too heavy for me to budge. So, in a state of disbelief, I stood waiting for Marc to return. "Well," he said, walking up a few minutes later, "will it do?"

"Marc! Where did you get this? What's going on?"

"Let's see." He seemed to be enjoying my confusion. "Yesterday you said that the whole display would be perfect, except that you needed artificial grass and didn't know where you'd ever find it at a price you could afford, right?"

"Yes, but—"

Marc cut in. "Now you've found it. Everything seems simple enough to me. But this stuff isn't going to do you much good in the middle of the sidewalk."

He hoisted it onto his shoulder and called out, "Katie, could you open the door to the store?" I was amazed at his strength.

I held the door open as he carried the bundle to the display. Then I hurried ahead of him and moved the trees out of the way. He set the Astroturf down on top of my cardboard and unrolled it. "Hmm, I don't think this is quite the right shape for the window. I'll have to cut it." He took out an X-acto knife. "I always come prepared."

"Marc, you've already done so much. Just tell me where you found this stuff. How much do I owe you?"

"This grass is rubber-backed and not easy to cut. Besides, installation comes with delivery. Do you want to cover the whole window floor?" I nodded yes. "A good decision," he said, and the next thing I knew he was down on his hands and knees cutting away.

I stood watching mutely. I wasn't sure which was a more perfect sight, my grassy jungle or the dearest, kindest guy I'd ever met working to make it all become a reality.

"Finished!" Marc stepped back to admire his handiwork. "Looks pretty good, if I do say so myself," he added.

"Good, it looks outstanding. Oh, Marc, how can I ever thank you?"

"No need, we're friends, right?" His eyes sought mine, and I wondered if he could tell that mine were glowing. "Catch you later."

"Wait, Marc, where are you going? I mean, that's none of my business, but I've got a great idea. If I work really hard this afternoon, I can finish this project by closing. Won't you come

111

back later and see what your artificial grass has done for the whole display?"

"Katie," he said, looking away from me, "you really don't have to act so grateful. I got the grass because I wanted to, and it was kind of fun to install. I'm not sure I can make it back tonight."

"Oh, well, I understand if you can't." Mentally I figured that he probably had a date again. I hoped it wasn't with the same girl. It was suddenly very important to me that he see the finished window. I wanted it more than I ever could have dreamed just a few days before. I certainly had no claim on Marc. I knew my window was going to be terrific, but it would mean much more to me if I could share the finished design with Marc.

I took a deep breath, "Marc, if you could stop by at all, it would sure be great. It would only take a few minutes, and I won't keep you from your other plans."

"Katie, I've got to run," was all he said.

I worked the whole afternoon, moving the bush and trees around, draping the jungle material just the right way, finding the perfect place for the pond, and finally selecting and situating each one of the animals in just the right spot. It was important that the placement both complement the overall effect and still show off the animal to be sold. At last, it was done. Monkeys hung from the trees. A crocodile swam next to a white swan in the pond. Frogs sat on rocks sunbathing. A lion peeked from one corner. My snake slithered toward the pond. And a family of bears stood by an opening I'd made to look like a cave.

Though the window was really finished without him, I picked up the teddy bear with the tear. He was my favorite, a kind of good-luck charm for me throughout the project. There were duplicates of every other animal, but he was one of a kind. Whoever bought him would be getting something very special. I put him off by himself, and it seemed as if he were looking wistfully after the other bears.

Finally I made a big sign, which I put in the back of the display. It read: "Warning! These Animals Are Dangerous—If Not Sold Immediately!" In smaller letters beneath that I wrote: "Do your part to keep ASU safe!"

I barely even noticed that the store had closed, that Jim, the cashier, had left, and that Mr. Tohn was in his office. I stepped out of the window to check the display from the street again, and on my way I glanced at the clock. It was seven o'clock already. Marc had never returned.

I stood outside, gazing at the display. It

was everything I'd ever imagined it could be, and yet, instead of feeling ecstatic, I was just standing there, wondering how long Mr. Tohn would stay so that I could pretend to continue working. I was still hoping Marc would show up. I went back inside and pretended to rear-range the animals.

A half hour later, Mr. Tohn came out of his office. I'd made him promise not even to peek at the window until I was finished with it, but he called, "Katie, I've got to lock this place up. You've worked hard enough for one day."

"OK, Mr. Tohn, come and see University Drug's jungle!"

"All right, Katie." He walked out the door, and I slowly followed him, half afraid of what his reaction would be. "Katie Thompson!" he thundered. Heart pounding, I wondered if he could possibly not like it. What if he wanted it taken down? But then I saw there was a big smile on his face. "Katie, this is a very profes-sional job. And it's positively unique. It's the best window display this town has ever seen. I want you to know I'm not a man easily impressed, but I'm impressed. Just wait until I bring Martha down to see her Cape Cod bay window!"

I was absolutely reeling from Mr. Tohn's

praise. He certainly wasn't a man to dole out compliments. Feeling great pride, I left the store with him and watched him close the door and lock it. Then he came over to me again. "Katie, congratulations. You ought to be very proud of what you've done."

I thanked him and watched him walk toward his home. I stayed around. I told myself I was just admiring the window, but to be honest, I was really hoping that Marc was still going to stop by.

Finally I had to face the fact that he just wasn't coming, and I said aloud for no one except me to hear, "Darn you, anyway, Marc Cook! How could you not show up tonight when I want to be with you more than anyone else in the whole world."

"Maybe it was because until now I never knew you cared," came a voice from behind me. An arm slid around my shoulders, and I looked up into Marc's deep brown eyes. He smiled and then, bending slightly, he brushed his lips against mine. "Katie," he said, his arm still tightly around me, "your display is perfect. By the way, I don't think it's going to work so well for us to be just friends."

"Me, either," I said, leaning my head against his chest and smiling.

Chapter Fourteen

Together, we stood arm in arm admiring the window display. "Katie, I'm not at all surprised that it's so terrific. I think all your hard work calls for a celebration. Can I take you to dinner, or did you already eat?"

"I'd love dinner," I said. "And it's our hard work, not just mine. Remember, you got the artificial grass. Where did you ever find it?"

Marc chuckled. "You know the saying—curiosity killed the cat. I'll tell you over dinner. Now, let me see, where can I take someone who is covered with green paint?"

I blushed scarlet. What a sight I must be. I'd worn some of my oldest clothes to begin with, and then I'd worked in them all day. I looked down at my knees. There were splotches of dirt on them from crawling around on the floor, and under the dirt areas of green peeked out.

I was really embarrassed. How could Marc stand to be around me in this condition? I asked him as much, and he answered, "Oh, I'm just a glutton for punishment." But he smiled and winked as he said it.

"I've got a great idea," I said. "Let's go over to my house. I'll clean up, and we can make some dinner there."

"Well," he said, teasing me, "there's always the chance that it's the green paint flecks in your hair that make you so attractive. But if you're willing to risk giving them up, it's all right with me."

We walked toward my house and that night, even the heat didn't bother me. I couldn't think of anyone or any place I'd rather be. As soon as we opened the door to the house, Mom came running into the living room calling, "Katie, did you finish it? I'll get Dad, and we'll go—" She stopped in midsentence. "I didn't realize you had company. Hello, Marc, it's nice to see you again."

Dad walked into the room. "Hi, Marc. Well, princess, how did it go?"

By now I was a little embarrassed. I didn't want to brag in front of Marc. "It went pretty well. I think it looks OK."

"OK!" Marc exclaimed. "It looks absolutely terrific! Katie's just being modest. Wait until you see it!"

"I can see that she certainly put her whole self into her work," Dad said. "Maybe Mom and I will take a quick run over to see the finished product."

"That would be terrific," I said, appreciating how much my parents cared. "I'm going to clean up a little, then Marc and I are going to make something for dinner." I excused myself and left the three of them talking.

Standing in my bedroom, I saw for the first time what a total mess I really was. If Marc could like me in this state, he really had to like me a lot. My heart absolutely sank with that thought. I ran in to take a quick shower and felt the layers of dirt and paint falling away.

Back in my room, I pulled a comb through my clean, wet hair and pinned it back. I threw on a multicolored sun dress and sprayed my neck with my favorite cologne. A little makeup, and I was a far cry from the state I had been in when I'd walked into the room. I shoved the clothes I'd worn under my bed. They were such a mess I decided they might have to be condemned.

I walked into the living room. "Wow!" Marc stood up. "I think Cinderella just got ready for the ball." I looked around the room to see if my dad was going to add some funny comment. "Oh, your folks ran over to see the display. They said they'd be back in a few minutes and that there wasn't much in the house. But they told us to help ourselves to whatever we could find. You know, my offer to go out still stands."

"That's OK. After all the hard work you did for me, the least I can do is get you some dinner." I thought to myself that I certainly had a lot of making up to do after the way I'd treated Marc when I'd first met him.

We decided to make spaghetti. The tomato and vegetable sauce was a little tricky to make, and I'd never done it before. But Marc had suggested it, so I didn't tell him I didn't know what I was doing. Besides, he was using this crazy Italian accent that kept me hysterical. The sauce we concocted looked good and rich. It began boiling, and I hoped Marc knew how to tell when it was done. Finally I ventured, "Here, you can serve the sauce up when it's ready."

"Katie, this Italian chef has-a no idea when de sauce is done. How-a do you tell?"

"Well, umm—oh, Marc, I don't know." The

two of us looked at each other and the mess in the kitchen and began to laugh. If the vegetables were a little undercooked, I never noticed. I could barely eat, anyway. I was too excited from my perfect day.

Mom and Dad returned, raved about my display, looked at the kitchen, and then decided to retreat to their room. "Don't worry," I called after them, "we'll get everything cleaned up."

"Yeah," whispered Marc, "it'll just take a couple of weeks." And we began to laugh again.

We began to wash the dishes together, and as we worked we talked. "OK," I said to him, "how did you come up with the artificial grass?"

"Magic?"

"Not good enough!"

"Oh, all right. It's really nothing too exciting. I've been working as a handyman on and off since the day I got here. After all, I have to have money to take you out."

"Come on, stay on the subject," I commanded, but I tingled at the thought that he planned to see a lot of me.

"Anyway, one of the ladies who I repaired a leaky faucet for was saying that she'd just replaced all the Astroturf on her patio. We were making conversation while I worked, and she told me that she'd had the old stuff carted off by some lady who owned an incredible secondhand store. So I checked it out today, and sure enough, the stuff was still there, hidden under a pile of junk that you wouldn't believe. I got the whole roll for three dollars. A friend of Dave's lent me his truck to cart the Astroturf, but only on the condition that I take it into Phoenix afterward and pick up some special seat cover he'd ordered."

"So that's why it took you so long to come back tonight. I just figured you didn't care that much and that you decided you'd already done your good deed for a friend."

Marc looked shocked. "Oh, Katie, I'd have been back to see that display no matter what else I had to do. But you see, I didn't want you to think I was coming on too strong. When I tried to show you I cared before, you froze me out totally. So this time I wanted to take things slowly. I planned to see the display. I was just waiting across the street until you left."

"Oh, Marc." My eyelashes were wet with tears. "You are the sweetest, most wonderful guy. I'm just so glad you didn't hate me for the way I acted."

121

"Katie Thompson, I don't think I could ever hate you." He pulled me close and kissed me gently. It was the moment I'd been waiting for all night.

Chapter Fifteen

I sat on my bed cross-legged and resolved that I wouldn't move until I'd written Sandy a nice long letter. She'd been so good about sending me letters, and I hadn't written her in weeks. I had so much to tell her. I mean, she didn't even know about Marc!

I began, "Sandy, wait until I tell you about Marc Cook. He is the neatest, most wonderful guy, and that doesn't begin to say enough good things about him. I'm enclosing several pictures. The first one is of Marc and me at a pool party."

Picking up the picture, I thought how different everything had been at this party than at the first one Marc and I had gone to together. This time, I walked in as Marc's girlfriend, and I was proud of it. In fact, I wouldn't have changed places with anyone there, especially not Cindy! I had my mature, sensitive boyfriend, and it didn't matter one bit what year he was in at school.

Dave had walked over to Marc and me that night, and patting my arm, he'd said, "I'm sure glad you two kids got everything worked out." As he sauntered away, I realized what a jerk I'd been. How could I ever have been willing to toss Marc away for Dave? There was no doubt that although Marc was a few years younger than Dave, he was already far ahead of him in sensitivity. I doubted if Dave would ever really be concerned with anyone but himself.

I put the picture of the party down and picked up another. There were so many, it was hard to decide which ones to send Sandy. My favorite was one of Marc alone. He had been totally unaware of the fact that I was taking his picture. He was sitting in an armchair reading and his hair was falling over his eye. He had an expression of studious concentration on his face. He looked handsome and strong, yet still vulnerable.

Of course, I had to enclose the picture of the two of us all dressed up. Marc had insisted on taking me somewhere fancy to celebrate my display. He'd arrived to pick me up wearing a jacket and tie. Mom had taken one look at the two of us and made an immediate dash for her camera. I planned to have a five-by-seven print made for my dresser. Marc looked absolutely wonderful, and I loved the way he was looking at me so tenderly.

I wrote and wrote to Sandy. Marc and I had had so many good times, and I wanted to tell her about all of them. "Well, Sandy," I concluded. "Though I miss you tons, I just wish this summer could go on forever. Every time I think about it ending, I feel sort of sick. I can't bear the thought of not being able to see Marc every day." When I finally finished the letter, I realized it was so fat I'd have to send it in two envelopes. Sandy would think that was funny, anyway. I labeled the envelopes Volume I and Volume II. On the way to work the next day, I put them in the mail.

Work had been going really well. Mr. Tohn's attitude had become considerably warmer, and I'd finally met his wife, Martha, who just couldn't find enough good things to say about the display. After three weeks Mr. Tohn was reordering stuffed animals, something he said he hadn't done in over two years!

One morning a rather striking woman walked into the store. I saw Mr. Tohn greet her warmly and gesture toward me. They walked over together. "Katie," Mr. Tohn said, "meet Dr. Ann Jenkins. She teaches marketing and display at ASU."

"Katie," the woman said, extending her hand, "I'm so pleased to meet you. Actually, you've been quite the topic of conversation in my class lately. I've heard so much about your display."

"Oh, thank you," I said, a little overwhelmed.

"No need for thanks. I'm impressed by what I've seen. I think you've got a lot of talent. You seem to have the creativity and understanding necessary for excellent advertising and display work." She opened a leather briefcase, took from it a gold pen and some paper, and began writing. "Here are some books you might enjoy reading. Do write to me when you're making a decision about college. Maybe we can even find a scholarship for you."

I basked in the compliments even after Dr. Jenkins was gone. Mr. Tohn saw her out, came over to me, and almost under his breath, said, "Katie, did I tell you how proud of you I am?" But before I could say a word he added, "The candy rack needs to be filled," and he walked away.

Stuffing the Nibs, Baby Ruths, and Milky Ways into their respective slots, I thought about what Dr. Jenkins had said. The future sure seemed filled with wonderful new possibilities. I still thought often of Katie's Clothing Boutique, but now I also imagined designing the displays for a big, fancy department store. Lost in daydreams of the future, it was no time before I'd closed the register and was waiting for Marc and our daily walk home.

As soon as he came in the store, I grabbed his hand and blurted out, "Marc, have I ever got great news!" Then I wished I could take the words back again. I could tell just from looking at him that something was really wrong.

"So what's your good news?" he asked as we started home.

"It can wait a few minutes." I tried to keep my voice light. "I've got a feeling you've got some bad news, and I always like to hear the bad news first. That way it's over, and the conversation gets better."

Marc laughed and let go of my hand. He ran his fingers through my hair. He sighed, and his smile disappeared. "Tonight, I insist you tell me your good news right now. I could use some cheering up."

So I told him all about Dr. Jenkins. "Well, it's nice to know the lady recognizes talent when she sees it," he said. "Someday you'll own Katie's Clothing Boutique, and it'll have

127

the best displays around!" I smiled. It was too far off in the future to plan for such a thing, but it was certainly something nice to think about.

When we got to the house, Mom and Dad were eating dinner. They'd gotten used to my going out with Marc or his joining us for dinner. Dad said that it probably evened out in the end because I was gone just about as much as the two of us showed up for dinner.

About a week before, Marc and I had finally gone to one of Dad's classes. I'd thought he was fantastic, but then again, he was my dad. Marc thought he was truly superb. "The thing that makes your dad such a good teacher," he told me, "is that he takes complicated things, explains them so everyone can understand, and still keeps them interesting." The other night Marc and Dad had quite a discussion about economics, and I was so proud of Marc. He seemed to understand a lot about it and to make his points well.

So just when life was absolutely perfect, something had to go very wrong. I didn't know what it was yet, but I could feel Marc's unhappiness. I wished he would tell me what was bothering him.

Mom asked if we were joining them for

tacos, and Marc woodenly replied, "I'm not really very hungry. I'll leave it up to Katie."

Marc loved food even more than I did, so I knew he was really upset about something. Figuring it would be easier to get him to talk if the two of us were alone, I opted to go out to dinner. Mom looked at me rather quizzically, since Marc looked so tired.

"OK, Katie, name the place." Marc smiled weakly. "Wherever you want is fine with me." His cheerfulness sounded forced.

I chose a quiet little restaurant on the other side of the campus. We could go there dressed as we were, and it was calm and dark, a good place to conduct an important conversation. We walked toward the restaurant in silence. Finally I couldn't stand it any more. "Marc, please. I know something is really wrong. Can't you tell me what it is? Maybe I can help you figure out how to make it better."

Marc's fingers interlocked with mine, and he took my hand to his lips and kissed it. "Katie," he said, "I'm leaving tomorrow."

The bottom had just dropped out of my world. "But—why? You weren't supposed to leave for at least another ten days. We should have over a week more together. Did I do something? Are you angry with me? Is that why you're leaving early?"

"Katie," he turned me to face him, "I shouldn't have said anything to you until tonight was over. I wanted our last evening together to be just as wonderful as all the others. But I was so miserable at the thought of leaving you that I couldn't act the way I usually do. I hate goodbyes, and this is going to be the worst one I've ever had to say. As for me being angry with you, believe me Katie, nothing in the whole world would make me want to leave you."

"Then why are you going?"

"My mother called. She says my grandfather is in the hospital, and Dad really needs some help in the hardware store. She didn't want me to cut my vacation short, but she was worried about what the long working hours were doing to Dad. As much as I want to stay here with you, I have to leave. Katie, please," he said, wiping the tears from my eyes, "don't make this any harder. We'd have had to do it in a few days, anyway."

I tried to stop my tears as they turned into hiccups. My eye makeup had either run or been wiped away, and I said, "Some romantic picture I'll leave you to remember me by."

"Katie," he begged, "let's just try to pretend this is any other night. Let's not spoil the little time we have left together." I nodded and took a deep breath.

Since neither of us really could eat anything, we walked into the restaurant and ordered root-beer floats. Marc sat with his arm tightly around me. There was so much to say that we just said nothing at all. Our bodies touching, we listened to the music and remembered. Eventually we made our way back home. *Tomorrow he'll be gone*, I kept thinking. Finally, I said haltingly, "I guess I should let you go pack." And Marc, eyes reddened and misty, agreed.

Gently he pulled me close to him, and his lips met mine. Then we stood back, looking deeply into each other's eyes as if trying to fix the picture forever in our minds. "I'll write, Katie," he said softly.

"Wait," I said, "I'll go to the airport with you."

"Katie, I couldn't stand going through another goodbye like this. Let's end our special summer tonight." His voice grew husky. He stared into my eyes a moment, gave me one last kiss, and then turned and walked away.

Chapter Sixteen

I couldn't fall asleep until almost four in the morning. When the alarm went off at seven, I couldn't believe I was supposed to get up and just go to work as if the world hadn't really fallen apart. My eyes were red and swollen from so much crying. As I lay in bed trying to gear up for the day, I knew I had to talk to Marc just once more. I didn't care what he'd said about goodbyes. I had to hear his voice again before we were hundreds of miles apart. Frantically I reached for the phone and dialed Dave's number: It rang. Four, five, six . . . ten times. No one was there. I was too late. Marc had already left.

I dressed and went to work with a heavy heart. How would I ever face closing time that day knowing that Marc wouldn't be waiting to walk me home? I was tempted to call in sick, but I couldn't very well play sick for the entire next two weeks, and besides, Mr. Tohn was counting on me. I sighed and wondered if I'd ever again be as happy as I'd been the last few weeks.

When I got to the store, Mr. Tohn called me over to the register. "Katie, meet Ellen. She worked for me all last winter. She's going to work mornings now and when school starts. Come with me, Ellen can handle the register, and you can check in some orders in the back."

For the next three hours I unpacked, sorted, and checked in new merchandise. As I worked I decided that as soon as I was finished, I'd go out and buy the little bear with the tear. After all, he was what had gotten me going on this whole project. I had bet Marc that he would sell right away, but I'd been wrong. After all those weeks, he still sat in the window. Strangely enough, we'd gotten duplicates of every other animal when Mr. Tohn had reordered, but not one of the bear. Well, he was a reflection of the way I felt right then. Nothing could wipe his tear away, and nothing could make me feel any better about Marc leaving. Still, at least I could hug my bear and think about Marc.

But when I marched out to the window to get him, he was gone! "Ellen," my voice was urgent. If only I had taken him before I'd gone to check in the orders. "The bear, the one with the single tear, did you sell him?"

"Yes. Wasn't I supposed to? Mr. Tohn said to check the stock first, and if we had none, just to sell the item out of the window."

"Who bought him?"

Ellen looked at me strangely. "Some girl. I don't usually ask customers their names before I sell them things."

Somehow I survived the rest of the day. As the dreaded moment of closing arrived, I heard footsteps come through the door. I was bent over the register, checking out the money, and for a moment my heart leaped. Then I remembered—Marc was gone. I looked up and standing before me was Dave.

The surprise on my face must have been obvious because he said, "Marc made me absolutely promise that I'd be here today at five-thirty to take you home." Unsure of what was happening, I followed Dave out the door.

Cindy was waiting in the car, and she moved over to make room for me. "It's really tough that Marc had to leave so suddenly," she said sympathetically.

I nodded, fighting the lump in my throat.

Dear, sweet Marc. He'd even made sure I didn't have to walk home this first night without him. In a couple of minutes, Dave pulled up to my house. I opened the door. "Thanks for the ride."

"Just a minute," Dave said. He hopped from the car himself, opened his trunk, and withdrew a large, white box with a letter attached to it. "Everything's here the way Marc wanted it," Dave said, handing the package to me. A moment later I was standing on the sidewalk alone.

"Open me first," read the outside of the box. I tore off the ribbon and pulled up the lid of the box. Inside sat my bear, the one with the single tear. He had a ribbon around his neck that said, "Now open the letter." I unsealed the envelope and began reading.

Dear Katie,

I already miss you, and I haven't even left yet. If all went according to plan, Cindy bought the bear for you this morning, and Dave took you home tonight.

Katie, I'll write lots, I really will, but I'd rather live in the future than in the past; so guess what—I've figured out that Duluth is exactly 153 miles from Minneapolis. Also, I've computed that homecoming is exactly fifty-four days from today. So, Katie, can you come and be my date for homecoming weekend? You can stay with my folks and me, and I can show off the most wonderful girl in the world to all my friends.

I hope you enjoy the bear. He's to remind you of me and to give you some-thing to hug until we see each other again. You said that nothing could make his tear disappear. Well, just wait until he sees the two of us together again.

Love,
Marc

I carefully folded the letter and hugged the bear. My special summer was over, but it would soon be the beginning of a beautiful fall.

We hope you enjoyed reading this book. All the titles currently available in the Sweet Dreams series are listed on the next two pages. They are all available at your local bookshop or newsagent, though should you find any difficulty in obtaining the books you would like, you can order direct from the publisher, at the address below. Also, if you would like to know more about the series, or would simply like to tell us what you think of the series, write to:

Kim Prior,
Sweet Dreams,
Transworld Publishers Limited,
61–63 Uxbridge Road,
London W5 5SA.

To order books, please list the title(s) you would like, and send together with your name and address, and a cheque or postal order made payable to TRANSWORLD PUBLISHERS LIMITED. Please allow cost of book(s) plus 20p for the first book and 10p for each additional book for postage and packing.

(The above applies to readers in the UK and Ireland only.)

If you live in Australia or New Zealand, and would like more information about the series, please write to:

Sally Porter,
Sweet Dreams
Corgi & Bantam Books,
26 Harley Crescent,
Condell Park,
N.S.W. 2200,
Australia.

Kiri Martin
Sweet Dreams
c/o Corgi & Bantam Books
    New Zealand,
Cnr. Moselle and Waipareira
    Avenues,
Henderson,
Auckland,
New Zealand.

Dear SWEET DREAMS reader,

Since we started publishing SWEET DREAMS almost two years ago, we have received hundreds of letters telling us how much you like the series and asking for details about the books and the authors.

We are getting to know quite a lot about our readers by now and we think that many of you would like a club of your own. That's why we're setting up THE SWEET DREAMS CLUB.

If you would like to become a member, just fill in the details below and send it to me together with a cheque or postal order for £1.50 (payable to The Sweet Dreams Club) to cover the cost of our postage and administration. Your membership package will contain a special SWEET DREAMS membership card, and a SWEET DREAMER newsletter packed full of information about the books and authors, beauty tips, a fascinating quiz and lots more besides (including a fabulous special offer!).

Now fill in the coupon (in block capitals please), and send, with payment, to:

The Sweet Dreams Club,
Freepost (PAM 2876),
London W5 5BR.

N.B. No stamp required.

I would like to join The Sweet Dreams Club.

Name: ....

Address: ....

....

I enclose a cheque/postal order for £1.50, made payable to The Sweet Dreams Club.

This offer applies to the UK and Ireland only.